W9-BAG-274

PLENTY PORTER

A Novel

PLENTY PORTER

BRANDON NOONAN

AMULET BOOKS

NEW YORK

Designer: Jay Colvin
Production Manager: Alexis Mentor

Library of Congress Cataloging-in-Publication Data:
Noonan, Brandon.
Plenty Porter / by Brandon Noonan.
p. cm.
Summary: As she turns thirteen in the early 1950s, Plenty Porter—the youngest of
eleven children—keeps some secrets and uncovers some dangerous ones as she tries
to understand her place in her family, town, and the world.
[1. Self-perception—Fiction. 2. Family problems—Fiction. 3. Secrets—Fiction.
4. City and town life—Fiction. 5. United States—History—1945–1953—Fiction.]
I. Title.
PZ7.N739434Ple 2006
[Fic]—dc22
2005021899

Printed and bound in Canada.
1 3 5 7 9 10 8 6 4 2

HNA
harry n. abrams, inc.
a subsidiary of La Martinière Groupe
115 West 18th Street
New York, NY 10011
www.hnabooks.com

An excerpt from *Plenty Porter* was first published in *Swink* magazine.

*For
Ellery Renger,
who is loved*

Prologue

*In which we meet Plenty Porter and the family
of ten other Porter children, and learn
the secret of her name*

PLENTY PORTER was nearly thirteen when her brother smacked her face red. I am Plenty Porter and my brother is Jerry and that was yesterday.

Now I'm upstairs in bed next to Marcie, who's saying, "Quit crying, Plenty, that was yesterday and there's no use crying about yesterday." But I hadn't thought about it all that much until now. Everyone else is sleeping, except Marcie, who is easily disturbed. Peggy, Rachel, Martha, Joyce, and Debbie are split up on two beds, all of us in the same room, but *where* I'm not sure. I'm only certain about Marcie, because she keeps sighing at my left. By the time the others made it upstairs and climbed under the covers, my eyes were already flooded. And now they're asleep and all I feel is the collective weight in the room. Of which I am not.

On Marcie's suggestion, I go downstairs, passing the room of my brothers—of Jerry who slapped my face red for scratching the hood of his Ford with a butterfly net, of Johnny, Bob, and Dean—who, with the six sisters, make ten. Plus one, who is me, and that is eleven. One more than a handful for each parent. There is one person who is too many, and that person is me. I pass the room of my parents—a room that is always half empty, different at day and different at night, depending on who is working. Then downstairs and outside to the porch where it is cool.

Across the road, a dim light wobbles inside a window on the top floor of the Prindergast place. That is Ed's room, I know, because I was invited inside once. Ed is in my grade and shares a bedroom with no one. His father owns the land we look after. He has no mother, because she died before he was old enough to need much mothering. He reads with a flashlight under the covers, the light dim, the light wobbling. Ed does not know that I am outside, that I am crying. Ed does not know because Ed doesn't need to think of those things outside his window, those things his flashlight touches when it wobbles, like me.

My father keeps a pack of cigarettes under a loose brick in the wall next to our mailbox. I caught him smoking one morning, and he gave me a quarter for the secret. I told him a quarter was a one-time payment, but if he kept smoking there would be more secrets to keep, more quarters to take. He said I'd be a rich woman for every cigarette he planned on smoking. We settled on one quarter a week. And I've kept the secret and learned to smoke, which he does not know, which when he does know, when he finds out, will be his secret to keep, and I will pay, or he will stop paying, and no money will pass between us. But for now it is not worth thinking about the future of our secrets, the secrets between my father and me, because it is nearly midnight, time to have a smoke and air out some before going back to bed.

The matchbook in my hand reads JUG'S in big, cursive, gold letters. I found the matchbook yesterday, the same day Jerry slapped my face red, at the same place, which is the school. There was a back-to-school dance that night and I helped decorate in the afternoon. I helped decorate because I wanted to help Marcie. The matchbook was on the floor outside of Marcie's locker. I wanted to help Marcie because earlier in the year Marcie had lost her hair, left school, and become something else entirely. But, again, all that was yesterday, and there's no use crying over yesterday.

It isn't until now when I peel back the cover of the matchbook, pull a cardboard match from the pack, and see Marcie's familiar handwriting written on the back I know that I've finally found a clue.

At this point decisions are made after I've made them. I am running across the road, feet sinking slightly into gravel, sinking with a certain familiarity because this is the path I take daily, usually in sunlight, but always barefoot. The thing about where I live, which is Alexis, Illinois, is that night is night, not like night in cartoons or movies, but night like it is here in Alexis, which is black. And so I am running toward the one thing I can see, which is Ed's room, the light in Ed's room which must be Ed reading; and it isn't until I am nearly up the tree and to his window that I realize I have been running since I stepped off the porch, that I made the decision to run.

I am asking Ed if he wants a cigarette, my voice full, my voice sharp. "Want a cigarette, Ed?" I say from a branch at his window. And Ed is startled, because Ed jumps and drops his flashlight on the floor where it rolls underneath his bed, leaving the room like the night, which is black; leaving me in the tree and unable to see anything but a glow along a floorboard. And then again I find that something has been altered, that I am standing inside the room much after I must have made the decision to jump from the branch, uninvited, into Ed's bedroom on the second floor of his two-person home, a decision I realized I made after I made it.

"Is that you, Plenty?" Ed is asking.

"Who else would it be?" I say.

"You should ask someone if you're going to smoke in their house," Ed informs me.

"I must've figured you'd just say 'yes' anyway," I say, which must be true even though I'm not sure.

"Your dad know you're out of the house this late, Plenty Porter?"

"He's at work," is something I don't say. I'm not sure if Ed knows that my dad works at night and sleeps during the day, so I don't say anything. Instead I pick up his book and start reading the first sentence of the first chapter, which is "Call me Ishmael," which I say out loud. "First person," I announce.

Ed laughs at me and says, "So what?"

"So, I don't like that person as much," I say. "I like talking about me like I'm someone else."

"That's third person," he says, which I couldn't remember but know is right when he tells it to me.

Then I am at the door to his bedroom, facing a long hallway, with a picture of his dead mother framed beside me, caught in a pocket of lamplight. Ed calls me back inside, "Shut the door before my pa wakes up and raises all hell." But I wave him off and only take one step into the hallway and stop; and once stopped, I only listen, which is to say I'm listening for something—snores or heavy breathing, an unconscious complaint. And it's here that it can be said I made a decision for the road. When you read the papers a few mornings from now and ask, "What would a little girl like her, like this Plenty Porter, want to do with running away at night, alone at night with only the risk of some Gentleman to come calling?"—which is what we call men like that, who travel on lonely roads looking to lure children with a black town car and fancy talk—then think back to this moment. I'm in the hallway listening for something, just before Ed beckons me back inside, which is now, which is what he is doing.

"Have you been crying, Plenty Porter?" Ed asks.

"It's nothing," I tell him. "It was only yesterday."

• • •

Somehow I am outside and limping. I made it to the tree branch, but missed the decision to climb, and fell. My knee is bleeding, and if you know anything about cuts, the hurt worsens as time passes; soon it will be stiff, making walking hard, running worse, and a car ride from a fancy stranger will be a welcomed change of pace. Because I am running and whoever finds me first, wins—use me as you please.

And so again through the gravel, sinking ever so slightly into the gravel, welcoming the dirt between my toes, away from the Prindergast place, away from the light in Ed's room, which is out now, which does not wobble and greet me on the street, which is not any sort of beacon; not like a lighthouse is to a man at sea, maybe a man like Ishmael on his way ashore through a storm in a book I haven't read.

And I am halfway down the road, alone in the road, when Ed comes from his house, through the front door in his underwear that is stained, something I don't notice now, but noticed then, upstairs in his room. He is calling, "Plenty, Plenty Porter, get back here, are you crazy walking barefoot and alone this late?"

And we are stopped together on the road. I am barefoot and he is half naked, the two of us, and all I can think to ask is, "Why didn't you take the tree, Ed? Why didn't you follow me down the tree?"

"I didn't want to fall," Ed says, "like you. I took the stairs and ran out the front door."

"Yeah," I say, "but it took you too long. I was nearly down the road by the time you made it. I'd forgotten that I wanted you to follow me by the time you started yelling."

"You wanted me to follow you?" Ed asks, covering himself for the first time. Hands cupped at his privates.

And he is twelve, but tomorrow I will be thirteen. And there is an answer to his question, and the answer is yes. But just yesterday Jerry slapped my face red. And once again I am crying, snot-dribbling sobs. And Ed takes off running back to his house, stopping only when he reaches the front door, to point and bark, "You're crazy, Plenty Porter," before shutting the door with a click. And again there is the road. And the two houses next to a field of corn that is theirs and not ours. And then a car. Somewhere down the road. A miniature double sunrise moving over the hill at the base of our property. Maybe a Gentleman coming to get me—those little girls and boys who stray too far.

But it is not a Gentleman. I recognize the sound. The sound my father's Dodge makes when it hits the gravel around the other side of our house. Usually the sound means morning. Tonight the skid and crunch, the crushing of weeds, is unfamiliar. Perhaps my father has come home to fetch me, or all of us, the twelve of us, away. And with that thought I run through the dark, before the spotlights catch me, to the other side of our house, and up to the porch and the cool. From the porch, I watch the headlights crawl under the house, through the basement, up through the spaces in the floorboards where I am sitting, as if he is driving up from underground, from inside the earth.

The engine cut, he makes his way around the side of the house and up the four steps onto the porch. I am on the swing, legs folded Indian-style. I have forgotten that I was crying. Forgotten why I was crying. Forgotten Jerry and his annoying red car, forgotten the obnoxious rise and fall of snores in my room and the next, of brothers and sisters—the ten of them of which I am not. His face is disappointment and fear, and that is to say that I recognize his face, that he has left work early and is not wearing a uniform, which is why I recognize his face, because it is mine, because for once I am not the only one on the outside.

Inside the house, the clock is chiming toward midnight. I count the number of *dongs* it makes and picture each of my brothers and sisters, in order of their birth. Bob first. Then Dean. By the time it reaches the number eleven, my head is as full as our house. The twelfth chime hits and I am thirteen years old. And seeing my father standing next to me, not noticing me, not hearing the breath of strain on the chain holding the swing, supporting himself with one hand on the banister, a drop of sweat collecting on his nose—about to break and drop—I see that it's us he will face on the inside. The eleven of us. Four beds. Two rooms. One house. No job. Numbers, not names. Is there such a thing as too many? I already know the answer. And the answer is the road. For me to leave, to travel along one road, then another, and not stop walking until I am sure I will never be found. For once it makes sense, my place in it all.

When Plenty Porter was born, she didn't have a name. Her parents had gone through all their favorites with the others. The doctor asked, "Think you'll have another?" Her mother kept the answer to herself. Her father said, "No, eleven is plenty."

I am Plenty Porter. I am plenty.

PART ONE

*In which Plenty Porter is nearly a year younger
than she was at the time of our prologue, and learns
about the gift of freakish height*

I.

PLENTY PORTER had just turned twelve when she realized that she had grown at least three inches too tall.

"Look at you," the other girls said on the day after my twelfth birthday, fingers pointing from inside the sleeves of their fancy-dancy dresses. "You're at least three inches too tall!" The day was Tuesday in Galesburg, Illinois, a day it was everywhere at the same time, except in Korea where it was already Wednesday, a fact that I've never really understood, how one place could be an entirely different day just by me not being there.

Galesburg is a town that is about thirty miles from our farm in Alexis, a town that is always bustling with farmers like us coming to sell and to buy from people who do not have to travel thirty miles in order to do such things. These people, like these girls who chase me through the streets, do not have to leave their homes to go places like Galesburg because they are already there.

"Look at her," they said, as if to one another but loud enough for me to hear. "She's so tall, she has to duck under the eaves."

I thought about the night. I thought about all the beds in our house during the night. I thought about thirteen people, twenty-six legs and feet, two of which are my own, dangling off the ends of the beds. And while I am not so tall to have to duck under the eaves of the storefronts, I knew that someday when I am as tall as my sisters and brothers, I will, because *they* do.

"She's too tall for this town," they said. "She's too tall for every town in the state!"

These are the other things, in addition to my freakish height, that the girls from town pointed out:

I am barefoot.
I am skinny.
My BVD undervest is stained yellow.
I am not wearing anything over my BVD undervest.
My hair is short and parted like a boy's.
I smell like a colored.

The last of these things I did not understand, because none of the coloreds who play music at the Apple-O smell any different than anybody else in the Apple-O, even though most of the people in the Apple-O are colored, which makes it sort of hard to compare one from the other—a fact that I wouldn't really think about much until later, when I was home and safe, curled into an afghan on the floor next to the radio, something my mother will call an *irony*, a word that I'll need defined.

My teacher, Mrs. Reynolds, always tells me to start my stories with something specific, "a taste of real life," as she calls it, even if that real life might be in the future and completely made up, or in the past and totally real, like this story just happens to be. For instance, this very morning my sister Marcie woke me with a handful of hair clumped in her hand. Marcie is sixteen and prone to picking fights, so at first I wondered which of our other sisters the hair belonged to, but the only crying in the house seemed to come directly from her, so I figured that the hair must be hers.

"Look," Marcie said once she had me alone inside the washroom, her stubby fingertips poking into her hair. I could hear her dirty fingernails scratching along her scalp and couldn't help but stare at the dead skin salting her shoulders. *"Look,"* she said again, and closed her fingers, catching a bunch of hair inside her fist. Then she pulled. I expected there to be some sort of sound, like shucking an ear of corn, a heavy tear, but there was nothing. Her fist came away from her head as easy as pulling seeds from a dandelion.

"Don't tell Ma," she said, the hair sitting loose in

her open palm. "Don't tell no one. It's nothing. It's nothing to talk about, Plenty, okay? You promise?"

"Promise what?" I asked.

"Promise not to tell!"

"Then why'd you show me?" I asked. "You know I don't know how to keep secrets,"—which is true.

"If you promise, you will. You won't break a promise."

"I don't know," I said, thumping my heel on the floor.

Marcie bent over and looked at me, forcing my eyes into the path of her own, all watery and scared. "Let me hear you say it," she said. "Let me hear you promise."

"I promise," I mumbled softly, which was a lie. And then I sneezed—something that happens when I lie, which everyone in my family knows. And were it not for the hair that suddenly scattered from her open hand and into the air, riding on a gust of my breath like a broken wish, Marcie would have recognized the lie. But instead she dropped onto the ground and frantically tried to gather up every last strand.

"Ma can't see this." She kept sobbing. "It'll scare her too bad!"

"Okay, okay, Marcie," I said, realizing that I'd better promise again and hope that it sticks. "I won't say nothing. I promise."

She climbed back to her feet and handed me the clump of dust-covered hair. "Here," she said. "You take it."

"Me?" I backed away from her and the hair in her hands. I was thinking about death. Pieces of us are always dying. Hair, skin, sloughing off and falling on the ground. Maybe Marcie was dying. Maybe my two brothers, Bob and Dean, who have left and will soon be fighting in a country and a war that are both named the same thing—Korea—maybe they will die. And the thought of that, of their bodies lying on the ground as limp as the hair in Marcie's hand, made me sad. And so I agreed to take the hair and do with it whatever she asked, even if the last thing I wanted to do was carry a piece of her, a *dead* piece at that, in my pocket all morning long.

"Okay, Marcie," I said. "I'll do whatever you say." And before the words had even settled in her ears, the door was shut and I was left alone inside the washroom, which for that moment was exactly where I wanted to be most in the world.

The washroom is a place I like to spend a good deal of my day because no one comes knocking or complaining when the door's been shut more than five minutes. My secret, though, is that an unfilled tin tub, when you're lying inside, makes noise sound distant; not *muffled* like when a pillow is stuffed over your head, but *distant*, like voices just before you wake from a long dream. That's the way I like to hear the sounds of my house and the people in it—sounds that were at that minute climbing up the stairs from the kitchen, where breakfast was waiting, and down the hall, reaching through the space between the door and the floor—like a dream I'm about to wake from and hardly remember once awakened.

But before I could make it inside the tub, everything went quiet downstairs. I heard kitchen chairs scooting on the floor and bare feet running for the backdoor.

Normally breakfast in the Porter house is like the joke where a family of, let's say, eleven, is done with dinner and there's still one pork chop left on the table. And for whatever reason the lights go out (as they always seem to do in stories like these), and someone screams. The father lights a candle and finds that one of his boys managed to grab the pork chop, but not before ten forks were jabbed into the back of his hand. And while I forget the moral of this story, I do know that this is exactly how breakfast, or any other meal, goes in our family. Turn your head and they'll take the food right off your plate. So when everyone gets up from the table before breakfast has even been served, it means only one thing: Someone must be driving up to the house.

By the time I made it to the one window upstairs that faced the front of the property, the visitor was already driving away onto the main road in a big black car, a cloud of dust snaking behind it like a gopher trail. Directly below the window where I stood, my family, the whole rotten bunch of them, was huddled together in a circle, staring down at something in my father's hands.

I ran straight down the stairs and into the kitchen,

where I could get a closer look at them through the screen door. Still in her apron, my mother hung on to my father's belt loop with one finger, as if that alone was holding her upright. Her lips were flapping without words. She was *reading* something over his shoulder. A letter! They got a letter and didn't wait to read it until I was around!

Jerry kept snapping at the stationery, trying to fetch it for himself, but came up with only a torn corner of the envelope. Peggy squeezed into the center of the circle by passing around Marcie (who was too busy scratching at her head to notice). Irritated at Peggy for stepping on his toes, Johnny kicked up some dirt onto her Sunday dress, which she always insisted on wearing no matter what day it was. Rachel and Martha took turns trying to hoist each other up onto the other's shoulders before letting gravity win, their big butts dropping back down on the ground—where they belong. And Father, tired of all the fuss, did exactly what he always does—gave up and pleased the crowd by giving them what they wanted. He read the letter out loud. And I couldn't hear a single damn word he was saying.

When the whole group of them came back inside the house a few minutes later, they found me sitting alone at the breakfast table, swallowing sausage links whole.

The drive into town takes nearly an hour. It might as well have been a year. No one would speak to me.

The letter was folded and stuffed inside the pocket of my father's overalls. Picking bits of sausage from the back of my teeth, my stomach turning from overeating, I wondered over the course of the long, silent drive if it was worth it—after all, I still didn't know what was written on that brown paper. But whatever it said, one thing was certain: It was important.

The back of the Dodge is a cramped and bumpy ride when all of us make the trip, and I am somehow always the last one inside, as if they half forget that I am making the trip (as if they half forget I exist), and I end up smashed against the gate, hardly able to breathe. But being that it was a Tuesday, I was happy for the unexpected trip. Something was about to happen. I could see it on all of their faces even though they wouldn't tell me what it was. We were leaving behind the fields and our schooling and the chores that "could not wait," as my mother always liked to say. *These things will not wait, Plenty Porter, it's your responsibility to feed Sadie and the other chickens, to do some of the milking, and they will not, cannot wait for a little girl like you to remember.*

But I always remember. I tell her this. *I always remember, Mama, and you don't need to keep reminding me. I don't need to hear it again and again. It won't make me remember any more or any less. I'm not a little girl anymore.* I tell her this, too. *I'm twelve years old now. In one year, I'll be thirteen. Don't you remember thirteen, Mama? You didn't have a mother when you were thirteen. And all you remember was hating her for all the things she never got around to saying. Remember? What do you want to say to me,*

Mama? Other than the chores? Isn't there something else that you want me to remember other than the chores?

I tell her these things at night, when my head is underneath a pillow and everyone else is asleep. Sometimes Rachel hears me when she's smoking at the window and tells me that if Mother knew I said such things, it would break her heart. She says that I don't understand yet what it's like to love someone so much that you hurt them. I don't understand why anyone would hurt someone they love, but she tells me we're not thinking about the same kind of hurt. The kind of hurt she's talking about is the kind that makes a person strong. But I don't always feel strong, I tell her. No matter how much hurting comes my way, sometimes I feel the other side of strong.

My father parked the Dodge at the top of a hill in Galesburg, and everyone jumped out and ran onto the sidewalk, not telling me where they were going, not inviting me along. They left me inside the back of the truck with nothing to do but climb out all by myself and muddy my bare feet on the dirt road 'cause no one warned me to bring shoes. They were on their way to deal with the letter that came in the post that morning, and I was barefoot and confused. And that was when I saw the girls who came at me in their fancy-dancy dresses, pointing and yelling at me that I am a freak because I am too tall. I yelled as loud as I could, "I am *not* too tall!" Even though by then I was quite certain that I was.

"Over here!" Someone was saying. My feet were sinking into mud and manure, as the sidewalks come to an end at some point, even in Galesburg. "Over here!" The voice was Charlie.

Charlie is a man I know in secret because he is colored, and I've learned it's better kept as a secret. I first met Charlie at the Apple-O—which is really just a restaurant with a juke that plays all kinds of music, except hymns—because Charlie runs the place. At one time in his life he used to stand outside from opening to closing time, making sure no person was ever met with a door shut in his face. But now he is too old for standing and sits in a rocking chair and holds the door open with his foot.

"Hey, Charlie," I said, watching the girls out of the corner of my eye as they turned back toward town.

"Bringing trouble with you, I see."

"Didn't bring nothing nowhere," I said. "Trouble just found me, that's all."

"It'll do that," Charlie said, "from time to time. I hear your folks had themselves a package in the post today."

"What package?" I asked, dropping down on my knees next to him.

"You don't know? You came all this way and you don't know?"

"'Course I don't, Charlie. I wouldn't be asking if I already knew, now would I?"

"You have a point there." He chuckled, rocking slightly in his chair. "Maybe they had a reason to keep it from you. Maybe I oughtn't tell you what I know."

"You better tell me, or I'll tell them you *wouldn't* tell me, which'll get 'em thinking since they don't know anything about you," I warn.

And this makes Charlie look sad, like the thought of him being colored and a secret had maybe slipped his mind.

"Please, Charlie," I said. "*Please* tell me what you know."

"Okay, Plenty, I'll tell you. Alls I know is that today's a good day for your mama. Today she gets her boys back."

At first I thought Charlie had lost his mind, and something on my face must have told him so, because he started laughing, which made me do something else with my face to show him I don't like people laughing at me.

"Now, don't go huffing and puffing at me," he said. "I'm not laughing at you. I just ain't never heard of nothing like it before, that's all."

"Like what?"

"Like one family having as much luck as yours."

"Luck?" I asked. "*Luck*?" I asked again, thinking I must have heard him wrong.

He leaned down to me, talking real slow and sweet, saying that nearly every young man in the state has been shipped off to war, and not a month later my two brothers got sent back. And why? 'Cause they're too tall to fit in the uniforms. Uncle Sam decided it ain't worth stitching up something special and so he sent them on home.

The sun was going down when I made it to the post office. It was cold and, were it not for the blood rushing to my cheeks from running, I probably would've wished I'd brought a sweater and my shoes. But I wasn't wishing for anything except to find my family so I could put them all in a line and do a count, just like Mrs. Reynolds does after recess to make sure all her children are accounted for.

Rounding one last corner, I found them walking a few yards ahead of me. I did a quick count, right then and there with their backs to me. And I came up with the number *twelve*. Charlie was telling the truth. There they were. My mother and my father and *all* of their children other than me, lumbering giants walking up the hill.

A bell rang from somewhere down the street, a shop door opening and closing, and I faced down the hill. The same four girls came from Kelley's Market in their fancy-dancy dresses, carrying cups of hot cider, jabbering on about something I could hardly hear, but could only guess was me.

A heavy breeze picked at my hair as brown leaves scattered down the muddy road and took flight, slapping against the girls who held their dresses down against their skinny legs.

And then I remembered—remembered the early part of the morning before the letter arrived. I remembered first my sister Marcie and then the secret waiting inside my pocket. And before the breeze died down, I made a decision to keep my promise.

Standing on the hill above the girls, with only the backs of her family to witness it, Plenty Porter, who was three inches too tall, lifted Marcie's dead hair into the sky and released it from her hand.

2.

"PLENTY PORTER is not sleeping, she's pretending," I said.

"Then Plenty Porter should also pretend to be quiet," Mama said back. "The rest will follow."

"What will follow?"

"Sleep."

"I don't want to sleep," I told her. Twenty minutes had passed since I was sent to bed. Mama had come to check on me. Downstairs everyone was celebrating. Father went to the cabinet and took out a bottle of his best drink—the kind that makes his lips pucker after a single sip—and not long after, I was sent off to bed. Mama opened the door quietly and found me curled on top of the bed in my overalls. I kept my eyes closed but could smell lye on dry skin and knew it was her. I was snoring, for effect, when she began to shut the door, so I announced that I wasn't sleeping, I was only pretending.

"Are you happy your brothers came home?" Mama asked, helping me into my nightshirt.

"Yeah, but why do I gotta be in bed when everyone else gets to stay up with them all hours of the night?"

"Because you're twelve, and freshly so," Mama was sure to add. She put her hand under my mouth and said, "Spit."

I chewed one last time and felt a piece of old gum snap against the roof of my mouth like a stiff twig. Jerry was the only one of my brothers to remember my birthday, because he was the only one I reminded. The gum came from his pocket, his last piece, but he gave it to me as a present anyway. Mama went to toss it in the garbage, but I asked that she set it on a napkin so it'd be waiting there for me in the morning. I figured she'd make a fuss about saving a two-day-old piece of gum, but she didn't. She placed the gum on top of the dresser and pulled back my blanket, saying, "It's time for bed, Plenty. Get under the covers and shut your eyes."

"Mama?" I said, before she shut the door behind her.

"Yes, Plenty?"

"Are *you* happy?" I asked.

Downstairs Dean was laughing at one of my father's jokes—probably the one about the Pope who made his driver let him drive his limousine through Rome and got himself pulled over. Mama heard the joke. Heard Dean's voice, so full that he easily could've been standing in the room, right there with us. And hearing this, Dean's full, pleasant voice, made Mama's mouth turn up into a moist curl, and I knew that the answer to my question, even before she said it, was yes.

Standing at the window a minute later, I took in the trees that surrounded the edge of our property and watched the branches respond to a sudden gust of wind. Already it was deep into fall and the trees had lost their leaves. Soon the cornstalks would turn brown and all signs of life would retreat below the ground as they got themselves ready for a cold, heavy snow. A flock of birds flew from the trees, black wings against a black sky, moving close together like I imagined locusts did back in the days of Moses. And turning my head to watch, I noticed a figure standing alone in the field, hands in pockets, regarding the same flock of birds. I knew the person to be Marcie, even though there was no specific detail easy enough to see from where I stood inside our house, behind a plate of foggy glass, to prove it to me. She stretched her arms above her head in a curious way, and I could have sworn that she was trembling. Without meaning to, I glanced over my shoulder, making sure I was alone in the room, making sure I was the only one to be witnessing my sister Marcie out there in the trees, trembling and alone. But when I looked for her once more, at the place near the edge of the field where she had been standing, she had vanished, and I was left to search for something, other than shadow, on which to fix my eyes.

• • •

The next morning, Mr. Prindergast came to visit. Even though he lived just a rock's throw away from our front porch, in a house that towers above our own, we hardly ever saw him, and when we did, it was such an occasion that everything at our home seemed to hold its breath, less in anticipation of the nature of his visit than in the hope of his speedy exit. In the past, Mr. Prindergast liked to criticize my father's handling of the crop. And his words, just like his visits, had the power to make my father walk slower, talk less, and spend hours out in the field, alone, kicking around his thoughts. But no harsh word was ever allowed to be spoken against Mr. Prindergast. My father was under the impression that no other landlord would keep a family as large as ours on his land, and in his payroll. "Mr. Prindergast puts each pea on your plate," he'd say, and make us count them. Once I came up with fifty-three peas, and Father said I owed Mr. Prindergast fifty-three "thank-yous." But I knew I'd never get up the courage to spit those two words out of my mouth when something as simple as "hello" was next to impossible.

"I'll be damned," Mr. Prindergast said, gripping both Bob and Dean around their shoulders. "I wouldn't have believed it if someone would have printed it in the newspaper," he said.

Of course, I thought, *no reporter would write an article about two Alexis boys getting to stay home instead of fighting in some war.*

Too many other boys in our area had gone off to fight for that to matter much.

"And to think," Mr. Prindergast continued, "I'd felt guilty for thanking God my Ed wasn't old enough to be drafted when you boys first got your letters." And he laughed. "Guess I didn't have much to feel guilty about after all."

Mr. Prindergast was not a tall man, but the shape of his shoulders—turned over like the curl of an aged newspaper clipping—made it possible to picture him as such some years ago. He was much older than my father, which always seemed odd since he had a boy exactly my age. Ed was his name, I knew because I heard Mr. Prindergast speak of him from time to time, just as Jerry spoke of his secret collection of arrowheads—something rare and special, kept safely away from the harsh, outside elements. I thought of Ed that way, like Jerry's precious arrowheads, because even though we were the same age, we didn't go to the same school. Ed went to the type of school that took driving to get to. Some mornings I'd see him climb inside his daddy's car with a stack of books bound by a leather strap slung over his shoulder. His was the kind of school that loaned out their books. My school was Alexis Middle School, just a half mile down our road. Alexis Middle School had the same collection of books sitting on a single dusty shelf, from which my mama had been taught to read some years ago.

We learned to read one sentence at a time. And being that school only lasted a few hours so that each kid could get back to their farm for afternoon chores, we never got through an entire book. We read sentences, sometimes paragraphs, but we never got to know what it was the writer might have been talking about as a whole. For this reason, Ed, with his stacks of books of different sizes and colors, a new book coming home with him each and every week, always seemed to be the keeper of secrets, like he was part of a club that us Porters would never get to join.

Mama brought Mr. Prindergast a fresh cup of coffee, and after one sip he spent the next few minutes trying to fish stray grounds off his tongue. Father joined my brothers and Mr. Prindergast out in the yard, and the four of them took a walk out into the field to "discuss the future," as Mr. Prindergast put it. Mama made me stay behind and watch them from afar. I couldn't hear a word they were saying. She went inside the house and I filled their flapping mouths with words of my own.

Mr. Prindergast, breaking a reed from a cornstalk: It's good to have you boys back home.

Dean: Good to be back, Mr. Prindergast.

Mr. Prindergast: Your daddy needs the help out here, 'specially in the spring when we try to make up for last year's misfortunes.

Father: Too much rain last year, late in the season.

Mr. Prindergast: Thing is, Ray, we can always find an excuse for our shortcomings, if we look hard enough for it. Hell, if I looked hard enough, I bet I could find an excuse out there right now, waiting to be plucked outta thin air, maybe one you hadn't thought of. But the thing is, I'm not looking for one.

Bob: But, Mr. Prindergast . . .

Father, cutting Bob off: Hold on, Bob, let me handle this. We worked hard this year, Mr. Prindergast, all of us, just as hard as any other year. Maybe harder. And each and every year you come on over and try talking down to us like you was our father and we was your sons. But it don't help any. Never has. We don't work any harder, or any less, after your visits. All we do is feel right nasty toward you, which makes us spend more time on our knees in front of Father Bishop, asking for forgiveness for our wicked thoughts, which in turn keeps us away from the fields, and maybe *then*, without us even knowing it, we do less work, and yield less of a crop, making you more upset, and then the whole goddamn cycle starts on up again.

Of course by then, Father was laughing at one of Mr. Prindergast's jokes, slapping his knee, and Bob and Dean followed suit, and I knew that none of the talk in my head was taking place. Mr. Prindergast was talking like he always talked, and Father was listening and nodding, listening and nodding, just like he always did.

The grove of trees next to our house is one of the places I go to play. One time Mama gave me and Marcie a nickel, and Rachel took us to the movies to see some picture about the old west. They opened the picture, though, with some old silent movie, which means there is music and the words are written on the screen. It was a movie about the future. In the future, airplanes will fly through the cities and weave between the big brick buildings just like cars. That afternoon, I came home and pretended the trees were the buildings and I was a plane. Now that I was hiding from Mama and had nothing else to do but stay hidden, I stretched out my arms like wings, shook my hands until my fingers became a blur like propellers, and tried to be a plane again. But the fallen leaves made the ground soft, not hard like concrete in a city, and the trees that had once seemed like skyscrapers now were crooked and made of bark, not brick. Suddenly, the whole thing seemed sort of ridiculous—me acting like an airplane. So I dropped down onto my back and wondered how it was I ever spent an entire afternoon pretending I could fly.

Digging my hands deep into a pile of leaves, I felt something cool and hard touch my fingertips. I couldn't tell what it was I'd found, so I made a game out of it and tried to guess. I kept my hands buried deep in the leaves and wrapped my fingers around the object. It was round and fit perfectly inside my palm. There was a hard point on the top and something long was attached to it. And just as I realized that something was a chain, I also knew that I'd found a pocket watch.

It was a new watch, not like my father's, which was

old and scratched and had been handed down from his father and maybe his father before him. It was gold, shiny gold, and not tarnished, which probably meant that it hadn't been on the ground very long. The crystal was clear, no water trapped inside, and the second hand clicked in perfect time. I put the watch inside my pocket and decided to keep it there until I found a hiding place for it. In less than a minute I imagined the total life of the watch, and with it, my own. I would keep the watch safe, away from my family, my brothers and sisters, for years, until the day came that I could pass it on to my own child. It would go to a little girl who looks a lot like me when I was her age, someday in the future when I am a mother and there is a father who is my husband, and the numbers in my age are reversed and I am twenty-one, not twelve, at the very least.

Running back to the house, it occurred to me, with everyone out and about doing their own thing, that a girl my age needs an ally. Someone she could tell about something like finding a pocket watch that didn't belong to her, and expect they'd tell her it's an okay thing to hold on to, even if someone else might be missing it. A girl my age, I figured, needs an ally to keep her from feeling guilty, which was how I was feeling when I made it closer to the house. As I began to worry that someone would notice the watch, or the bulge it made inside my pocket, I knew that a secret, unless it was shared with at least one person, can also be a lie.

I chose Marcie to be my ally because she'd trusted me with one of her own secrets the day before and because she was standing alone with the chickens, far enough away from the house that no one would hear what it was I had to say: "Hey, Marcie," I began.

"You didn't feed Sadie," she said, and walked away. Feeding the chickens was my daily chore. With all the excitement of Bob and Dean and Mr. Prindergast and now the watch, I'd forgotten to feed my favorite chicken, which I told her was the case. "I don't want to hear it," she said, and scratched her head with one finger like a monkey.

"I got a secret, too," I told her.

"What do you mean, 'too'?" she asked, stooping over me.

"You know, you told me your secret, so I thought maybe I could tell you mine."

"I didn't tell you any secret," she said, and walked farther away, deeper into the chicken coop, sprinkling seed on the ground.

I followed after her and said, "Sure you did, just yesterday, remember? You told me about your hair."

Marcie turned around sharp, and I could tell she was angry with me. "Just forget about it," she said. "Everything is fine now."

"But . . ." I said. "It was only yesterday."

"A lot can change in a day," she said, and her voice cracked.

"Okay, Marcie," I said. "Okay." We stood there a while longer, not talking. I could see Mr. Prindergast across the road, back at his house, climbing up the steps to his porch. Already the mood had changed around our yard, like everyone had finally let out the breath they'd been holding all morning long. *The time for telling secrets has passed me by*, which was something I thought as I climbed over the fence, leaving Marcie with the chickens.

I joined Jerry and Johnny inside Jerry's jalopy.

"What are you doing?" I asked them from the back-seat.

"Jerry thinks he's going to get his car to start," Johnny said.

"It'll start," Jerry said. "Just needed a little love."

Johnny laughed as Jerry put the key in the ignition. Johnny said a short prayer for the car. "Dear Jesus . . ." he began as Jerry popped his knuckles and grabbed the key. Jerry took a breath and gave the key a good turn, pumping the gas pedal to feed the sputtering engine. A tight fist of black smoke shot out of the tailpipe. Bob and Dean dove to the ground like they were taking cover from an attack and rolled on their backs, laughing. Jerry kept turning the key, kept pumping the gas. The engine rolled and finally turned over like a miracle. Inside my pocket, the watch slid off my thigh, and I could feel it ticking against my leg like a heartbeat.

3.

JERRY DROVE US to school that day, me and Johnny. There were always cars in our yard, coming and going, and I never really knew which one belonged to which brother or sister. Someone would get a summer job and suddenly a new car would appear. Father would spend the next afternoon or two under the hood trying to get it to run, sometimes without luck. Rachel was the only one of us who actually needed a car, because she was going to school to become a nurse. She saved up for two summers for a Buick that actually ran, and father kept it running as if it were his own, paying out of his own pocket for parts. He told us all that Rachel paid him back by being responsible enough to save for a car that was reliable.

Bob and Dean shared father's truck and seemed content in doing so, but always kept their eyes open for a "good deal" to mention to Jerry, because he loved cars more than any of us, not for transporting, but for racing. Jerry spent most of his time and money looking to buy the car with the biggest engine, and sometimes would have two or three of them up on blocks at a time. But when winter came, most of his cars wouldn't start because of the cold. Soon they would disappear into the snow, not to be seen again until spring, when they'd reappear, rusted and ruined. Those cars would be sold for pennies to Bill Baker, who owned the junkyard. Bill would strip them down and resell the parts to mechanics in Galesburg. Father said those same parts, most of them damaged, probably ended up in the same cars that his kids, desperate to waste their summer money, would see on the side of the road with a FOR SALE sign posted in the dusty back window, a deal "too good" for someone like Jerry to pass up.

We pulled up to school, bringing with us a roar that shook the windows of the schoolhouse. Mrs. Reynolds covered her ears as Johnny and I climbed out. "My brother drove us to school today!" I yelled to her as we ran up the path. Jerry kept the car running and lifted the hood to proudly inspect his handiwork. Mrs. Reynolds scurried over to him and ran her finger along her neck like she was cutting open her throat. Jerry nodded and got back inside the car to kill the engine. A moment later, it was quiet again.

"Mr. Porter, aren't you going to be late to school?" Mrs. Reynolds asked Jerry as I joined my friends next to the swing set. I figured Jerry wasn't planning on going to school that day, not with his car up and running again. He'd likely spend the day emptying the gas tank on the roads between our house and Galesburg, which Mrs. Reynolds probably knew herself since she spent the next five minutes crouched down next to the driver's side door, holding on to the frame so Jerry couldn't drive away, giving him a good lecture like she did when he was a boy.

That morning, the grandfather of a boy in my class played four instruments at once. He was visiting from out of town and he was dressed like a pirate. I knew this to be part of his costume when he peeked from under his eye patch to get a better look at the distance between his foot and the drum pedal. But I wondered where he came from, what kind of place teaches a grown man to play four instruments at once instead of farming or factory work? As it was explained by Mrs. Reynolds, we were in for a "special treat," because this grandfather had just come from the *Queen Mary* cruise ship, sailing from New York to a place called Europe, doing his one-man-band routine on Saturday afternoons. He beat a drum with his foot, played a banjo in his hands, blew through a harmonica held by a wire in front of his mouth, and even struck a cymbal with a little rod glued to the middle of his forehead. It sounded like noise to me. But the kids loved to dance, and he provided some sort of rhythm. Of course, Mrs. Reynolds loved it the most. Ever since her husband died at the hand of a colored fellow, who just happened to be my friend Charlie's son, she loved to talk to men from far-off places (like the man who brings us paper products; she does her hair up every time he's scheduled to come, and he's only coming from Chicago).

"I wish I had a grandpa. Then Mrs. Reynolds would like me the most," I told Johnny at recess.

"You do have a grandpa, same one as me."

"But that's not the same. He's never been anywhere good."

"What are you talking about? He's from Ireland. That's something, ain't it?" Johnny said.

"I don't know. You think he'd ever come to class and flirt with Mrs. Reynolds?"

"No, Plenty. I don't."

"Why not?"

" 'Cause he drinks and lives with the coloreds."

My cheeks burned like red-hot coals. I could feel my pulse beating in my ears. Everyone on the playground who heard Johnny was now laughing and snickering at me. They were thinking, *She's the girl who has family living up close and personal with the coloreds.*

"Why'd you go and say that?" I asked Johnny under my breath.

"It's true, isn't it?" he asked. The fact was, I had no idea if it were true or not. None of us kids had ever met our grandpa on our mother's side, which was the only side that had a grandpa still living. Our grandpa was alive; we'd seen him once or twice, collectively, on the streets of Galesburg. But Mama and him never did get along too well and so he was never invited for

Christmas supper, not once. He was a drunk who lived with the coloreds, just on the other side of the river, right next to the mill. Those things add up to something that his coming from Ireland and struggling ever since couldn't possibly erase.

In the afternoon, we worked at art tables, side by side, doing arithmetic. I could still hear them snickering, every one of them, even though they'd stopped by the time we made it inside the classroom after recess. I hated counting past ten. The problem in front of me involved the division of fractions, which seemed ridiculous—dividing something that already was not whole. I went over each number with my pencil, covering the page with my body so that Mrs. Reynolds might think I was hard at work. I was not thinking about math, but of the pocket watch still inside my pocket. It was a comfort after such a bad morning. A boy in my class had a respectable grandpa who played music on top of the ocean, but I had a pocket watch.

Thinking of all these things, I did not hear Mrs. Reynolds when she asked if I was having trouble. "Are you having trouble, Miss Porter?" she asked again.

I kept my head down, kept scratching at the page, and mumbled, "No, ma'am."

She tapped me on the shoulder twice and told me to sit up straight and quit slouching, so she could get a better look at my work. I pulled back my shoulders and felt my shoulder blades pinch my spine. Other than doodles, the page was blank. Sunlight glared off the lead-covered numbers. Mrs. Reynolds came around the other side of the table in two big steps. She dropped down onto her knees and we were face to face, with only the table between us.

"Miss Porter, are you lying to me?" she asked in a way that didn't need an answer.

I shook my head no. Which was when she slapped me. I took note of my surroundings: of the chalk dust that clung to a beam of daylight in the corner of the room. Of Sally and Lucy and Tracey and Billy, so many classmates with y's at the end of their names, holding their heads down so as to not bring trouble their way. Of the sound the slap made, which was, to me, the sound of a cheap tin cymbal. Of a single teardrop, or spit that splattered and soaked into the page that was empty of the equations and numbers, which caused the slap. And then, the uncomfortable quiet that quickly overtook the room. The sting came later, on the walk home. For now there was only her face staring back at me, waiting for me to say something, my teacher, not that much older than my sister Rachel, who was becoming a nurse so she could help people—Rachel, who would never slap a patient, who had never slapped me.

When I didn't say a thing, she asked, "Are you going to cry?"

I shook my head no.

"There are no breaks in this classroom," she said. "No one gets off free."

• • •

I waited in the outhouse after school, wanting to walk home alone so I could cry, which was my plan and had been throughout the rest of the day. Through the slats between the boards I could see my brother Johnny walking with his friends down the road, reenacting the slap. Johnny was playing Mrs. Reynolds, I could tell, because he pretended to push up on a pair of spectacles. He pulled back his hand and slowly brought it down on Sally Tripper's face. Irritated, I looked away and flipped through the pages of the JCPenney catalog. Half of the pages had already been ripped out and used as toilet paper. Somewhere within those pages was the toy section, balled up and dropped below into the foul-smelling hole beneath the outhouse. Not interested in reading about tools, I took a pee and waited for the voices outside to fade away.

Once I could again hear the flag flapping up on the flagpole, I snuck out of the outhouse and started home. At first the road felt like the start of an adventure. This same road traveled past our farm, through Galesburg, into Springfield, and beyond the state of Illinois. If I kept walking, if I didn't turn right on Shanghai Road, which is where we live, there was no telling where I'd end up. Dark clouds collected in the sky like blue dye dropped into a bucket of water.

At the end of the road, which to me was as unthinkable as the sky, it was probably raining. Walking a few yards farther, I could almost make out individual gray streaks blurring the horizon. *Maybe,* I thought, *maybe today is a bad day for running away.* Which was when I felt the sting spread along the left side of my face, as unexpected in its delay as the actual slap had been. Even without a mirror I could trace an outline of Mrs. Reynolds's palm, each finger, where they had landed, and realized that sometimes something that happens once can happen again in memory, and be worse or better, depending.

"Get in," Jerry said.

He saw me in his rearview mirror, stopped, and waited at the side of the road until I walked past the open window. Once inside, he asked why I was crying and I told him that Mrs. Reynolds had slapped me for no reason and that I hated her.

He slid up in his seat so that his legs were straight and he could fit his hand inside a pocket. He pulled out a hanky for me to wipe my nose. "Here," he said, and made a sudden left turn.

"Where you going?" I asked.

"Going to go see your teacher," Jerry said. We were driving pretty fast when he made another left turn, taking us right back to school. "If someone's going to be so mad as to hit you, Plenty, the least they can do is calm down and explain to you why."

The closer we got to the school, which was only a block from the house Mrs. Reynolds shared with her mother, the more I felt sick to my stomach. "I don't want to," I told Jerry. "Just take me home. I don't need a reason for it."

"Sure you do," he said, and fumbled with a pack of cigarettes.

"Hand me one," I said, holding out my palm.

Jerry looked over at me with a smirk that seemed to say he didn't think I knew how to smoke. I kept my palm held out in front of him. Finally, he slapped the pack in my hand and I removed a cigarette. He lit his own with a Zippo and kept the flame burning. I leaned forward, the cigarette pressed between my lips, and let the tip stab in and out of the flame, sucking until malt-flavored smoke filled my mouth. I sat back hard in the seat and swallowed. Jerry watched me out of the corner of his eye. I knew he expected me to cough. He didn't know that I'd been secretly smoking for months, even though I sometimes purposely lit up on the ground next to his car, hoping he'd come outside and find me. I held the smoke in my lungs until it burned, and exhaled through my nose. "Thanks," I said.

Jerry said, "Damn . . ." and tapped ash out the window with his index finger. We'd arrived at Mrs. Reynolds's house, a small box the size of Mr. Prindergast's garage, with a steep-sloped roof built up inside the branches of an old oak that would outlive us all. "Damn," he said again, and I realized he wasn't talking about me.

I waited inside the car while Jerry joined Bob and Dean out on the porch of Mrs. Reynolds's house. I figured Jerry was asking why Bob and Dean had come to her home. It did seem queer that all of us would end up together at the same spot. But when the screen door opened up and Father stepped outside wearing his Sunday jacket, I knew that Mrs. Reynolds must've phoned our house to talk about her troubles with me.

Mrs. Reynolds came to the door but did not step outside. She held the screen door open and said hello to Jerry before the four of them started back to their cars. I felt a lump rising in my throat and did my best to swallow it down before Father saw me inside Jerry's car. But he didn't see me, or he made like he didn't. He kept his head down and walked right past the window, past me, and got inside the Dodge with Bob and Dean.

Jerry opened the door and slid behind the wheel. Mrs. Reynolds took a step onto the porch as Father drove away, and knocked away some cobwebs on the eave above her front door.

"I'm in trouble, then?" I asked Jerry as Mrs. Reynolds turned back inside and paused, just long enough for me to see that she had been crying.

"No, you're not." Jerry said.

"No?"

"No."

4.

IT WAS HOT the day of the funeral.

Mrs. Reynolds's mother was a Methodist, which meant that her church had chairs instead of pews and a cross up front that was missing a Jesus. Father thought it best that we wait out on the street until the church was filled so we could stand in the back and not take thirteen seats away from their friends and family. It was Saturday. There had been a wedding the night before, and the ground outside the church was still littered with uncooked rice and wilted rose petals. I thought of the procession into church like a wedding in reverse, all the guests sucked back inside, forced to experience something sad, as if they were being punished for too much celebration the night before.

This was not the first funeral I'd been to, not even the second. I'd been there when Mrs. Reynolds buried her husband, Arthur Reynolds, one summer past. We had stood in a line to greet her at the graveside, Mama and me, and I worried what there was to say to a widow who would also be my teacher a few months later. Mama told me to smile and say, "I'm sorry," but that didn't seem to be enough. Turned out there was nothing for me to say, because Mrs. Reynolds spoke to me first. She put her hand on top of my head as Mama spoke some Scripture, then looked down at me and said, "I look forward to having you in class next year, Miss Porter."

This year it was her brother Ben who had died. On the way to the church, I asked Rachel, "Who done it?"

"Done what?"

"Shot Mrs. Reynolds's brother." As usual I was the only one talking. Rachel wore her nurse's outfit, hoping, I guessed, to look official. *Too late for nurses*, I thought. *The boy's already dead.*

"No one *did* it," Rachel answered.

"How could *no one* shoot someone?" I asked.

"Well, someone did, but there's no way of knowing who," Rachel said, shifting her body away from me.

Mama was driving Rachel's car, all the while keeping her eyes on father's Dodge driving ahead of us with the boys. "It was the enemy, Plenty," Mama said. "In a war, that's all there is to know."

There it was, the truth of it. Bob and Dean didn't have to fight in a war, because they were too tall, and Mrs. Reynolds's younger brother died because his height was average. I heard Mrs. Reynolds's voice ringing inside my ears after the slap. *No one gets off free.* But we did, us Porters. Bob and Dean got off free while, in one year's time, Mrs. Reynolds lost both a husband and a brother. And somehow I ended up paying the price. I got slapped and Mrs. Reynolds got to feel a little bit better. For a second, I didn't mind it all that much.

There are many different ways to grieve, and usually each way has something to do with how the person died. I'd now been to three funerals, each one different, but all of them had something to do with someone from the Reynolds family. Mrs. Reynolds's husband, Arthur Reynolds, was killed in a fistfight with a colored teenager. Two days later, that same colored teenager was found dead next to Shanghai Bend, just a half mile downriver from our house. Arthur Reynolds was a friend of my father's because they grew up together.

It was during the funeral of my father's best friend who died in a fight with a colored boy outside of a tavern that I first saw my father cry. Because Arthur Reynolds was Irish and a Catholic, his funeral was held at St. Joseph's Church, and it was full to the brim with angry people, most of them Irish, grieving with their fists in the air. "Arthur Reynolds was a good man," more than one person said from the pulpit. "Arthur Reynolds was a good man who was murdered."

When it was his turn to speak, Father said simply, "My friend is not with me today," and came back to his seat next to Mama, which was when I first saw the tears.

That evening, father woke me from a nap and carried

me out to the car, half sleeping. We took one of Jerry's newest purchases, an old Chevy, mint green, that Father had finally got running that morning. We drove twenty minutes into the hills, just over the river, to a gathering of cabins built from scraps of wood near the mill. I knew this to be the place where the coloreds lived—people like Charlie who owned the Apple-O, although I'd never actually been there. It was also the place where I supposedly had a grandpa.

When we got out of the car, I noticed another funeral was in progress. Up ahead was a flat bit of land where a church had once stood and burned, leaving a blackened outline on the ground where grass refused to grow.

"Why don't they got walls to their church?" I asked Father.

"They lost their walls," he said, knowing that I was now even more confused.

How does someone lose four walls? It occurred to me that there were many mysteries about colored folk that I would never fully understand.

"Hush now, Plenty. This is a funeral."

Father took me inside the far edge of the black dirt and held my hand tight in his. My friend Charlie walked right by me, saying nothing as he passed down the wide space between two sides of log benches, to the front of the church where a pine box sat on the dirt floor. I wondered if he didn't want my father to know we were friends, which seemed strange since we'd come all that way. Charlie kneeled in front of the box and started wailing in the key of G, like he was crying and trying to sing both at the same time.

Father picked me up like he did back when I was small, which I was then, and I said to him, "Everyone looks so sad."

Father said, "They are, Plenty. I want you to remember this when your friends at school start talking out against Charlie's boy."

"It was Charlie's boy who got killed?"

"It was. I lost a friend in Arthur, but Charlie lost his son. And there ain't nothing worse than losing family."

On the way home, Father said that it's good, sometimes, to make yourself see the other side of things, even when you don't want to.

Just under two years later, at the funeral for Mrs. Reynolds's brother, we stood again in the back of a church, this one with walls and a roof, and listened as the pastor gave a sermon about the power of prayer. I saw the back of Mrs. Reynolds's head bobbing as she held her mother's hand, nodding along to the pastor's message. "Everything in this world is made up of a cause and an effect. Ain't no different for prayer," he preached. "If the body of Christ has a cause, then the body should come together in one place to pray, to hold hands, and petition to our Savior for an effect!"

The Baptists sighed and said "Amen," the Catholics crossed themselves, and the Methodists looked over their shoulders, trying not to make mean faces at the strange rituals of their guests.

To me it seemed like an odd sermon for a funeral, because the pastor looked awfully mad. I thought that maybe this Methodist pastor was angry at us, the people of Alexis, Illinois, because we knew the Reynolds boy and maybe could have kept him alive with our prayers. Maybe he blamed us. Or maybe he just didn't know what to say to a congregation of people, not all Methodists, who were there to grieve something that happened in a way that none of us could really get hold of in our minds. How to picture a boy we knew in visions of cornfields, yard work, and the unloading of boxes at Harvey's Paint Company, now in a place none of us had ever seen, killed by an enemy with no face, and no name other than that of a place?

Because of all this, the air in the church was confused, not angry like at Arthur's funeral, or sad and scared as it was for Charlie's boy. Mostly it was hot. I pulled at my lace collar and tried to unfasten the top button, but Mama slapped my hand away.

"It's rude, Plenty," she said, "to show your discomfort at a funeral."

I nodded and leaned back against the wall, hoping to stop the trickle of sweat traveling down my spine by soaking it into my dress. But not long after, as the pastor kept talking with no sign of stopping, the women started to fan themselves, one by one, first with their hands, then with their programs. The men took up the rhythm a bit later, as if they'd gotten permission from the women, and soon all of us stirred the air together, like we were one body, not in Christ as the pastor would have liked to believe, but in some sort of shared, common need. This, above anything else having to do with cause and effect, made sense to me. The people were hot. The people fanned themselves.

The night of Charlie's boy's funeral, I came home and fell fast asleep in Father's arms as he carried me up to bed. Not long after he set me onto the mattress, I was prodded by fingers and woke to find each of my brothers sitting on the floor next to my bed.

"Did you see him?" Jerry asked.

"Who?" I asked.

"Grandfather. He lives up there, you know."

"I don't think so," I said drearily.

"How could you not know? It's like finding a pea in a plate of macaroni."

"I didn't see him," I said.

"Did you look?"

"No," I said.

"How could you not have looked? You were right there."

Johnny chimed in, "Maybe he changed colors. Like a lizard. Maybe he looks brown now." Jerry hit Johnny in the arm for being stupid.

I thought of Charlie at the funeral—thought of his face, the sacks underneath his eyes, the jowls under his chin. He looked limp, his face, his shoulders, as if the stuff inside of us that keeps us stiff, that keeps our faces together and our shoulders high, had drained out from his fingertips the farther he walked down the aisle toward the pine box where his son now lived.

Being that we were the last people in the Methodist church, we were the first outside and the first to form a line to wish Mrs. Reynolds and her mother well as they followed the casket to the cemetery. A bunch of boys from the Army showed up and brought their rifles with them. I was looking at them, wondering how they stood absolutely still without itching or shifting in their boots, when Mrs. Reynolds came by and touched my left cheek, right where she had slapped me, while Mama spoke to her another bit of Scripture. Mrs. Reynolds looked down at me, just as she did at her husband's funeral, looking ever so sad. But this time I spoke up first. "It don't hurt at all, Mrs. Reynolds," I told her.

And she said, "I'm glad, Plenty. I'm glad."

It was the first time she said the front side of my name.

5.

IT WAS RAINING that day, a terrible downpour, so I knew I was bound to get muddy from feeding Sadie and the other chickens. Instead of shoes and a raincoat, I chose to go barefoot and unprotected into the rain and mud. This would save me from having to clean off my shoes after breakfast, and would give me more time to play. Sadie was shivering under an eave outside the barn. Her feathers were pulled tight around her body, as if she'd traded them in for a pelt.

Some days I considered Sadie my friend. She listened as I fed her. And I rewarded her with games. I strung her seed in looping lines throughout the yard, giving her exercise as she ate, which I think she appreciated, because she'd usually let me pat her head afterward—much more affection than she'd allow anyone else in our family to give her.

But today it was cold and I was muddy up to my knees, so I dropped a heap of seed in a wooden dish under the eave and told her I was sorry before running back to the house.

Before breakfast, Johnny walked in on me, alone in my bedroom, my feet freshly cleaned, playing with the watch. I was sitting on the floor between the two beds, a blanket spread over the gap like a roof. He bent down at the entrance to my fort and saw the watch in my hands. Before I could get out a single word, he snatched it up and was on his way down the stairs, swinging it by the chain, calling, "Mama!"

I ran after Johnny, trying to get him to listen when I said that I wanted to show it to him last month, but he was too close to the house and I was afraid someone would hear. But he wouldn't stop running down the stairs to listen. I missed a step with the heel of my foot because of the water that had suddenly filled up around my eyes, making the edges of the stairs blur like a fast-moving river. I tumbled flat onto my backside and was crying even harder when I said, "It was a secret, it was my secret," over and over again, even as Mama took the watch from Johnny and asked where it was I found it, and who it belonged to.

"Me," I answered, thinking of the little girl my age who would someday be my daughter, who now might never have a pocket watch handed down to her. "It belongs to me."

Mama found Father outside next to the barn holding himself to keep out the chill. It had been raining for three days, and the fence that lined the corral had washed out due to thick, flowing mud. He'd been outside all afternoon digging holes deep enough to hold up the fence posts, only to watch them get filled with mud and rainwater within seconds of withdrawing his shovel. The stand of trees that created a grove for me to roll and play and lie in the fallen leaves and find secret objects hidden deep inside during the summer rolled and swayed in the wind above Father and Mama like heaps of bones held together by string.

Mama left the door open when she came back inside and told me to put on my rain slicker and go see my father. I told her, "It's okay, you can keep the watch, I don't want it no more." But without her having to say much of anything, I was escorted outside. She shut the back door behind me, and I felt rain drum against the vinyl skin of my slicker.

Father waited for me next to the barn. He lifted a fence post from the ground and propped it against the barn door. I saw that his hands were bloated and blue and that he was shivering. Hoping to change the subject away from the watch, I asked, "Why don't you go inside? It's cold."

"I have to get this fence up before the horses get it in their heads to leave the barn," he said.

There was probably more I could have said to keep us talking about things less important than being in trouble for holding on to a watch that didn't belong to me, but nothing came to mind, so I rubbed some water out of my eyes and blinked until I saw things clear again.

"You know, Plenty, keeping a thing that doesn't

belong to you without telling anyone about it looks a lot like a lie. I wouldn't want to think that a daughter of mine would lie."

"But . . ." I said, "but none of you asked me about a watch, so how could I have lied about having one?"

Father looked disappointed. "Now, Plenty, you know well enough that a fine watch like that doesn't belong in the hands of a girl your age. The Christian thing to do would have been to find out who it belonged to and get it back to them."

"But nobody I know carries a watch, 'cept that hunk of junk you and Bob share. Who do I know that has a watch like that?"

"Do you want me to tell you?" he asked.

Father was looking across the way at Mr. Prindergast's place. I turned and faced the house. Smoke poured out of the chimney like fog creeping up over a canyon, only to scatter suddenly into the wind. Father kept his eyes on the house, waiting for me to figure it out on my own. *The watch belonged to Mr. Prindergast. Of course it did. Who else could afford to buy something like that?* Father saw in the oval my mouth made that I understood.

"So why don't you take the watch and bring it on over to Mr. Prindergast's house. Tell him you found it a while back and realized the right thing to do would be to give it to him," Father said.

He dug into his pocket and pulled the watch out by the chain and stuffed it inside the pocket of my slicker before it got too wet.

"Go on, now," he said.

I knew there was no talking him out of it, but the thought of having to say all those things to Mr. Prindergast made me sick. I started walking slowly across the yard, daring myself not to stick my hands in the pocket and feel the watch, which is what I wanted to do most. But I knew something like that, feeling the one possession that ever meant anything to me, would get me crying, and crying would make it even harder to get any talking done with Mr. Prindergast. So I gripped the bottoms of the sleeves of my slicker and tried my best to ignore the watch as I stepped onto the wide porch of the Prindergast place.

There were stories I'd heard in school about war. Men were gone, sent thousands of miles away from their homes to fight in muddy trenches, and their wives were left behind to look after the homes, tend the fields, survive the winters. Mama told me this when I was little. She told me that no matter what the trouble, a girl could always count on other ladies to help her through tough times. Back when Mama was little and her mother was already dead, her daddy had to go off and fight and she was left to call on strangers for aid. Women like Mama could march up onto the whitewashed porches of the well-to-do women, and—just by them being female—they got all the pies and meats they could eat.

For a second I wished it was Mr. Prindergast who had died, leaving behind his wife to raise their boy, Ed. Then it'd be a lady I'd be calling on to return the watch. A lady would welcome me with warm cider and, in front of a crackling fire, share a good laugh over the whole thing. And maybe, just maybe, that same lady, the one who would have been Ed's mama and Mr. Prindergast's wife, had she not died, would have sent me home with the generous gift of the pocket watch still inside my pocket. "A girl like that Plenty Porter," Mrs. Prindergast would say to her girlfriends, "deserves the spoils of a lady, since someone as smart and witty as she will someday, undoubtedly, be one herself."

I could hear music scratching from a record deep inside Mr. Prindergast's house. The voice was a soprano, and her music, so high-pitched, licked the insides of my ears in an awkward tickle. By the time I got up the nerve to ready my knuckles for a knock against the door, a young boy began talking to me. It took me a while to realize that all this time he'd been watching me from inside the house, sitting on a chair next to a window, a window that was open just slightly.

"Are you ever going to knock?" the boy asked.

I moved away from the door, slowly stepping to the far side of the porch where a bench sat underneath a window. I knew the boy to be Ed Prindergast, even though his position inside the house, behind a fogged-up pane of glass, made him very hard to see. The window was only open a couple of inches and Ed sat with his head laid out sideways against the sill so that most of what I saw was his nose and mouth. I asked, "What are you doing sticking your nose out the window like that?"

"My pa says that we need to keep the cold out, so he

closed up all the windows and struck up the furnace real high. It's hot as Hades in here," Ed said.

"Why don't you ask him to turn it down some?"

"Because I have asthma. Pa thinks the cold will settle in my lungs and make it hard for me to breathe," he said, sniffing in a bit of cold air like a prisoner begging for food from the space under his cell door.

I lowered myself down onto the bench and asked, "Do you know my name?"

Ed stuttered some, like maybe he was scared of getting it wrong and offending me. He began to make the sound of an *m*, saying, "Muh . . . muh . . ." and I knew he was thinking of Marcie. I used my pointer finger to spell out the letters of my name in reverse against the fogged-up window. By the time I got to the letter *e* he remembered and called out, "Plenty!"

The music stopped inside the house, the soprano no longer tickling my ear. Ed's pa hollered, "What'd you say, Ed?" from somewhere in the back of the house. "Did you say something to me?"

Ed jerked up from his place behind the open window and pushed the frame down from the top. I looked back out at our house, through a curtain of water pouring down from the outer eaves, and saw Father still next to the barn, working with the corral fence. I thought about heading home and pretending to have given Mr. Prindergast back his watch, but I knew Father would check to make sure the job was done before letting me inside. I pulled the watch out from my pocket and set it down on the porch just outside of the front door. I could knock and then make a run for it, but the thought of Mr. Prindergast accidentally stepping on the watch when he walked out onto the porch made me pick it back up again. I knew my only choice was to knock on the door and see the whole thing through to the end. Which is what I did right then.

Mr. Prindergast made the mistake of thinking I was there to visit with Ed, so he let me inside and led me into the library where Ed was sprawled out on a blanket in the center of the room, as if he was having a picnic on a beach next to some lake on a day that wasn't so cold. In fact, it was so hot inside the house that it might as well have been summer. Suddenly, I wished I could take off my slicker and my sweater and get down into my underclothes. But doing such a thing in a house like the one in which Mr. Prindergast and his boy, Ed, lived alone, among fine furnishings and portraits of old men in fancy black suits, would probably be rude, so I plopped down on the floor next to Ed and whispered into his ear, "It's cooler down here."

"That's because heat rises," he told me. I spent the next few minutes wondering why then Hell was below the earth and not above.

Mr. Prindergast came back inside the library with a newspaper and sat on a brown leather couch that seemed to fart as he settled across from us. I started giggling, but stopped when Ed rolled his eyes and asked in a mean-spirited way, "Why are you here?"

"That's not nice, Ed. Miss Porter is your guest. We treat our guests better than that," Mr. Prindergast said while trying to turn to the next page of his paper, only managing to wrinkle the pages into a ball.

The last thing I expected Mr. Prindergast to do was defend me, especially since I was a Porter. He'd always seemed to think us Porters were nothing more than hired help, which we were, really, but here he was making sure Ed treated me like he would any other visitor to their home. I could tell Ed didn't like me being there—he seemed jittery and I wondered if maybe he was afraid I'd tell his pa that he'd had the front window open. Of course, it did seem strange that I'd be sitting there on the floor, next to Ed, without any questions asked, especially since we'd never played together, never been to each other's houses. Ed and I weren't friends, but right off it was like Mr. Prindergast thought we were.

"Why don't you ask Plenty to help you out with that crossword, Ed," Mr. Prindergast said.

"You're doing a crossword?" I asked.

"I *was*," he said, pulling out a workbook with a glossy cover, and flipped through the pages until he found a half-complete crossword puzzle. He pulled a pencil out from behind his ear and began filling in the boxes, one letter at a time, while I looked over his shoulder and tried to figure out why it was the letters he put together made no sense. It wasn't until I realized he was writing more than one word per line that I saw he had written a message. *Go home*, it said.

I grabbed the pencil out from his hand, figuring it was my turn, and wrote: *Why?*

Because.

Because why?

Don't need a reason.

Yes, you do, I scribbled, this time in the margins of the page, outside the maze of small boxes that made up the puzzle.

He followed my lead, filling the page with the words, *I don't have to like you if I don't want to.*

I started to respond but was so angry that the pencil couldn't keep up with my mouth and I was shouting, "No wonder you don't have no friends!"

Ed jumped up from the floor and pointed at me, saying, "That's a double negative. Tell her, Pa!"

Mr. Prindergast set the newspaper on the couch cushion at his side and stood up, telling Ed to hand him the workbook. Ed folded his arms stubbornly and turned his back to the room. "It's okay, Mr. Prindergast," I said, still sitting on the floor. But he bent down anyway and picked up the workbook and read our messages.

"You owe Plenty an apology, son," Mr. Prindergast said. "You had no reason to write these things."

But Ed did not apologize right then. Instead, he ran from the library and straight up the stairs. I sat on the floor and listened as his feet thumped along the floorboards, finally resting in what I guessed was his bedroom directly above. I started to get up when Mr. Prindergast dropped the workbook on a table and said, "My boy thinks I force friends on him. He gets embarrassed easily, I think. I hope this won't keep you from calling on him again."

Mr. Prindergast was leading me away from the library, down the hallway that ran alongside the staircase, and I saw the front door directly in front of us. Once again I could hear the rain. And just as I had the thought of walking out the door, of leaving the house and the horrible heat that was trapped inside, I felt the tick of the watch inside my pocket. I'd forgotten the point of the visit. I knew if Mr. Prindergast opened that door and left me standing outside, it would be nearly impossible to get up the nerve to knock once again.

I paused at the bottom of the stairs and looked up toward Ed's room. Mr. Prindergast had his hand on the front-door knob. Turning to him quickly, I said, "Do you mind if I try saying g'bye to Ed?"

Mr. Prindergast smiled and said, "Okay."

Ed was in his room lying on top of his bed, a bed hardly wide enough to hold more than one person. I stood at his window, looking outside to the side of our house, while I figured out a plan. Ed could see nearly everything from his room—our barn, the pump, the yard that spread around three sides of the house; he even had a slight view of the cornfield. I thought about how lucky he was to get to see so many things at once, where most of the time I was stuck seeing things as they were through my eyes only, some five feet up from the ground. *Maybe*, I thought, *he'd seen enough of me from up in his room to know I wasn't worth being his friend.* And suddenly I was a little bit sad. It was like the time Peggy had brought her new friends from camp to the house and they picked me last for dodgeball, just because they'd seen me trip over one of Jerry's toolboxes and figured I was clumsy without really knowing it to be true. "I'm not clumsy, Ed," I said, and turned to look at him.

"What are you talking about?" he asked.

I could've explained, but Ed and I had some business to get to. So I wiped some sweat from my forehead and opened things up by commenting on the tree outside his window, "That tree's good for climbing. You could open that window and sneak outside and your pa would never know it."

"I don't climb trees," he said, burying his head into a pillow.

Walking around the side of his bed, I grabbed the pocket watch out from my slicker and dropped it down on the bed next to him. He peeked his head out from under the pillow and seemed confused until I told him that I was willing to make a deal.

"I promise not to come round no more if you take this watch and tell your pa you found it someplace he never would go looking. That way I won't get in trouble for holding on to it for so long. It'll be our secret," I told him. "And you won't ever have to see me again, 'cept maybe outside if we go passing. But even then I won't so much as look in your direction. Cross my heart."

Ed wanted time to think about the pros and cons of our deal, as he put it. I paced his room while I waited, looking at all of his things, surprised that he didn't have more toys or games. His room was spotless. The walls were empty—no hangings or decorations, except a picture of a woman wearing a modest blue dress buttoned up to her chin. She seemed half asleep. That is what I thought as I approached the frame. It wasn't until I brought my finger up to the glass, ready to touch the thin line of her upper lip, that I saw the faint trace of a smile, as if it were about to blossom, just before the picture was taken.

"Don't touch that!" Ed snapped.

"Who is it?" I asked, my finger still poised at her face. Ed took three big steps and grabbed my hand, squeezing it hard.

I stepped away from the wall, suddenly afraid, as if Ed had saved me from some terrible trouble I did not quite understand.

"It's my mother," he said.

Ed turned and grabbed the pocket watch in his hand. Just as I was about to protest, to beg him to keep the watch and go along with my plan, he dropped it into his pocket. And just like that I finally had an ally, just like Marcie had one, unknowingly, in me.

It didn't occur to me that Mr. Prindergast had left his house until I made it home and found him sitting at our kitchen table.

Mama said, "Go on upstairs, Plenty. We're talking with Mr. Prindergast now. I'll call you down for supper."

Marcie was sitting on the stairs, secretly listening, when I rounded out of the kitchen. "You steal a watch and look what you get," Marcie said as I passed. "That's what I hate about you, Plenty. No matter what kinda crap you pull, your life always ends up sugar and candy."

I didn't stop to ask what she was talking about, because as I moved farther up the stairs I saw her run her chewed-up fingertips along the back of her neck. A chunk of hair was missing just at the base of her skull. It left behind a flaky bit of gray scalp, hidden partially by the longer strands that dropped down from the top of her head. By the time I was inside our bedroom, Marcie had slid down two steps closer to the kitchen and did not notice that I was staring down at her from the doorway. I suppose I felt a little bit lucky—the only thing I had lost was a watch.

The fort I'd built earlier in the day was still stretched between our two beds, although the sheet had sagged some. I heard the loose cannon of our heavy kitchen door forced shut into a swollen frame and went to the window to watch Mr. Prindergast hunch over and jog across the yard, avoiding puddles, until he was out of sight. Mama was coming up the stairs. I knew this because she is the only one who stays to the sides of the steps where there is more bracing, keeping the wood from moaning in discomfort. Mama says the last thing she wants is for the stairs to make comment on the effects of her giving birth to eleven children, each of them pushing eight pounds.

Knowing that Mr. Prindergast had yet to be given the pocket watch I left with Ed—since Mr. Prindergast was walking over to our house at the exact time me and Ed were making our deal and had not been home since—had me scared that Mama was on her way up the stairs to wear me out for not doing what it was I was told. For this reason I dove into the fort between the two beds and threw a blanket over my legs. I'm not sure why it was I felt the need to take cover. Mama rarely took a hand to me, and even when she did it was mostly for show. But something about the watch, Mr. Prindergast's watch, had changed things. For the first time in my life, something I did was causing havoc in the lives of my folks. And this fact had me scared, had me hiding in a fort waiting for something to come my way, something terrible, brought on by nothing more than a silly object that kept the time. And as Mama made her way down the hall toward my bedroom, I started to wonder how it was that a watch ever got to be so important to me. What does time have to do with a day in the Porter house? From one hour to the next, one day to a week, a month to a year, does anything really ever change?

Mama opened the door and light spilled in from the hallway, casting a pink glow inside the fort. "Plenty," Mama said as she shut the door behind her, making everything inside the fort seem dull and colorless.

"Plenty," I said back.

Mama lowered herself between the two beds so I could see her, or at least a part of her. Scrunched down with her knees at her chin, Mama looked like one of those little people who rewards tigers for jumping on a beach ball in the traveling circus. "What did you say, honey?"

"Plenty," I said again.

Mama squinted some, not quite sure who I was talking to, or why I was repeating the sound of my own name. It was not that there was someone else in the fort with me, no imaginary little girl bundled in the blanket at my feet with the name of Plenty, but for the first time the thought of trouble, of discipline, of punishment, made me back away and become, somehow, nameless.

Mama said, "Plenty," but there was no Plenty in the room. There was only me.

"I have good news," Mama said.

"For who?"

"Well, for *you*," she said.

"For me," I tried to say, but settled on something simpler—good or bad news, the up of finding a watch and the down of losing one, it was easier to stomach when it happened to someone else, to *her*, the girl with that name; even when the news was good, it was easier, "for Plenty."

6.

THE FIRST BOOK I ever read was given to me by a nun. That same nun had become my teacher like this:

She had become my teacher out of chance, not out of expectation, not out of anything that really had much to do with me. She became my teacher because Mr. Prindergast said she could be, that he would pay for her to be my teacher, and that he would drive me (and Ed) to and from her each and every day. That was the good news Mama gave me. Mr. Prindergast would pay for me to go to the same school as Ed, to be taught by the same teacher.

The teacher's name was Sister Helen Rose and I learned quickly to love her, mostly because she had so many books in her classroom. They filled shelves that lined the south wall; they were stuffed into desk drawers and cabinets, and stacked on the floor. Once I found three books in the coat closet, deep inside the pocket of her winter coat. I asked her then, Sister

Helen Rose, my teacher, who was a nun, "Why didn't you become a librarian?"

She told me, "No need going to a place that has all kinds of books when you could collect them all yourself."

"But it looks to me like you're running out of space."

"There's lots of room in the convent," she said.

"Closets and such?" I asked.

"Yes, Plenty, there are lots of closets in the convent. I have two in my room."

"Still," I said.

"Still, what?"

"Seems like you'd have more if you were a librarian."

"Doesn't really matter. Only one book *really* matters," she said.

"The Bible?" I asked.

Sister Helen Rose shook her head up and down, like she was thinking about other places, far off, and said, "I guess."

St. Joseph's Middle School was in Galesburg, Illinois, which meant I had to get up extra early every day in order to make it there on time, which was eight o'clock. Mr. Prindergast's car would be idling outside and I'd run from our house with an arm in only one sleeve of my coat because I was scared he'd be mad if I made them late. But Mr. Prindergast was never mad, because he never got around to talking much in the car, which meant he never told me he was mad—so I naturally assumed he wasn't. Ed and me would sit together in the backseat, the front seats occupied by Mr. Prindergast and his satchel, which was brown and worn and full of papers. For the most part, none of us did any talking.

On the first day of school I asked Ed if he liked St. Joseph's.

He answered, "It's fine," without turning in his seat, without looking at me.

This was how it was every morning we drove to St. Joseph's. I saw the side of his face, never the front, never both his eyes at the same time.

Not long after I started attending, a first snow came our way, which made Mr. Prindergast drive slower, which meant earlier mornings and a longer time in the car; a longer, silent drive spent looking at things that never looked back at me.

The first day was the easiest because I spent it getting measured for a uniform. I found one that fit in the waist but not in the length; the skirt was too short for my legs, which were too long. I was told that fabric would have to be added to the bottom of the skirt, but wouldn't be ready until the next day, so I'd have to spend the day alone in the dean's office while the other kids, whose legs were not too long, sat inside classrooms with books.

St. Joseph's was a large white building situated next to the Catholic church that shared the same name. It was one block away from Corpus Christi High

School, which is where I'll go if I ever get to be that age—presuming that Mr. Prindergast would still take me there. "St. Joseph's and Corpus Christi used to serve all grades, but St. Joseph's was an all-girls school, while Corpus Christi was for the boys," Mother told me the night before. I'd been to Corpus Christi with Marcie many times because it had a gymnasium and a swimming pool. We'd been there so many times one summer that the priest in charge of physical education gave us our own two lockers and said we could keep 'em year round. Hers was locker number 512, and mine was 513, and I felt good about being one number higher.

The halls of St. Joseph's were painted yellow and were lined with crucifixes of all shapes and sizes. It seemed to me that the men who made these statues were in a great disagreement over how it was Jesus looked on the cross. On some of them, he looked like he was in a lot of pain and was even bleeding from his hands, feet, and a small gash at his side. On others, he seemed less in pain, but simply irritated by the nails that were stuck through him, like, if the nails were to be pulled out with the claw of a hammer, he would simply walk off and have a meal—well, another meal, I guess—with his twelve friends (minus one).

We stopped outside a classroom in the center of a long hallway that looked out on a courtyard with a statue of the Virgin Mary, her body covered with weeping wet ivy. Before being led to the dean's office for my afternoon alone, I peeked through the window in a door and saw a classroom with a handful of students my age. Ed sat in the middle of the room. I watched Ed and thought how funny he looked to be in the middle of things and yet so far on the outside, both at the same time. When the other students laughed, Ed would lift the top of his desk and pretend to search for a pencil, as if he had more important things to do than laughing.

The teacher, who I would later learn was Sister Helen Rose, who I would later learn to love, was a young woman not much older than my oldest sibling, Bob (who was in his twenties, who "should be looking for a wife," as Mama says). She was standing to the side of the chalkboard, telling a story—the kind where your hands wave and your body hops up and down. She wore all black, with a white hood (a "habit," I would later learn), and a rosary that dangled from her neck like a puppet on a string. It seemed so ill-fitting that a woman who could make so many expressions with her face would be a nun and not a performer, like the woman who traveled with Roy Rogers and his horse, Trigger, when they came through town last summer. That woman had gotten everyone singing and dancing, and even made some jokes with Dale Evans, just before they brought out Trigger, which was just before I touched his mane and swore to never wash my hand again. That woman was most certainly not a nun, but this nun was most certainly a performer.

And just before the door opened and two girls

came from the room looking to go pee, I saw the most amazing thing I think I'd ever seen up until that point in all the twelve years I had lived.

"Who are you?" the girl I would learn was Annie asked.

I was watching the door slowly swing shut, watching the inside of the classroom that would be my classroom, and did not realize that the girl, Annie, who was asking my name, was the same girl from Galesburg who had called me a "freak" for being too tall. I was staring into the classroom, even after the door had fully shut and the window narrowed my view, because inside the classroom was a collection of books more massive than I'd ever seen. There were so many that there was no order. They were stacked, piled, shoved into nooks and crannies. The nun who was escorting me to the dean's office was introducing me to Annie and Sarah, two girls who had called me names and chased me through the streets of Galesburg, but I was thinking only about books.

"Plenty? What kinda name is that?" Sarah asked.

The nun blocked the window with her penguin body and said, "Don't you want to say hello, Plenty? It isn't polite to be rude."

"Are all those books mine?" I asked.

"What books?" Annie asked, but I wasn't looking at her, I was looking at the nun because she knew the answer.

"The ones inside. Are all those mine?"

"No, they are not," the nun said. "They, just like

everything in this school, belong to God, which means they belong to us. Just like you, Miss Porter. You, now, belong to us."

On the morning of the next day, my second day at St. Joseph's, I was given a new skirt to change into and was told by a nun, as I dropped my overalls to the ground, revealing my dirty knees, being from *my* station, and getting my schooling here, made me a "very lucky girl."

I played with the skirt on the way to class because it was different than all the other girls'. A three-inch strip of wool fabric had been sewn to the bottom of the original skirt with a jagged, uneven stitch in order to get it down to the middle of my calves, which, I learned was "proper," especially for a girl who was "*afflicted* by having so much leg," as I learned that day I'd been.

The girls from town, Annie and Sarah and the two others I had not yet met, were standing at the far end of the hall, waiting for Sister Helen Rose to unlock the door. Sister Helen Rose was jiggling a set of keys, making no real headway, and I knew that time spent outside the room, and outside of Sister Helen's control, was time that could easily be spent in ridicule.

They would say, "What's wrong with your skirt?"

"It's because she's so tall!"

"She looks ridiculous!"

And I would say, "Yeah, she sure does!" And they would get really confused because, well, who was *I* talking about when they were talking about *me*?

"Who are *you* talking about?" they'd ask.

And I'd answer, "Plenty Porter! Who else?" And it would be like the saying Father sometimes says—*If you can't beat 'em, join 'em*—whenever he had to do something that went against his nature. I would join them in making fun of me.

Of course the thought of actually doing that, saying those things, taking a stand against myself, as if I *were* someone else, seemed crazy even to me, so I slowed down and walked like I was running underwater. By the time I finally made it to the classroom, the door was open and everyone else was waiting inside.

I knew I had a friend when Sister Helen Rose got me involved in a game of jump rope with Annie and the girls.

We were inside the room where they stored the mats for gymnastics. During the winter months it was cleared out so that the kids would have a place to go at recess when it was snowing too heavily outside. Sister Helen Rose saw that I was sitting alone in the corner of the room with a book—one that I had borrowed from the shelf in our classroom and had been trying to read all day.

"Plenty, why don't you go play with the other girls?" she asked.

"I'm fine."

"I'm sure you are," she said.

"I am."

"But why don't you?"

"Why don't I what?" I asked.

"C'mon, Plenty. Don't be stubborn."

"I'd rather read," I said.

"So would I."

"Then do it."

"I can't, I'm your teacher. What kind of a teacher would I be if all I did was sit and read?" she asked.

I thought about that some. "So," I said, "you're saying that everyone has to do things that they don't want from time to time?"

"Yes. From time to time, they do," she said.

"Well, you should probably tell the other girls that, since the last thing they'll want to do is invite me into their games."

"Do you know that to be true?" she asked.

"Yes," I said, "I know that to be true."

Sister Helen Rose was looking at the girls with the jump rope for quite a while before she said, "How about I make you a deal?"

"I like deals," I said.

"Well, good. Let's make one, then. How about I let you take a book you want home every night, all the way through Christmas, so long as you keep bringing it back in good condition?"

"Okay! What I got to do?" I asked.

"*You* have to get into that game of jump rope without me helping you." Deals didn't seem as enticing after that. "What do you think, Plenty?" she asked.

"Any book I want?"

"That's right. Any book."

I handed her the book I'd been reading and got up. Ed was watching me out of the corner of his eye, but I pretended not to notice. He'd been busy throwing a dodgeball against the wall and catching it, which seemed pointless. "What are you doing?" Ed asked me as I walked across the room.

"Getting me a book."

"From where?"

"Just watch and you'll see," I said.

Two girls, Jenny and Sam, flipped two ends of a rope while Annie and Sarah took turns dancing in and out of the eggbeater-shaped arc the rope made. They were chanting as they jumped to a rhyme I'd never heard before, which was odd since I'd been jumping rope since before I learned to jump, if not sooner.

Lucy left the light on late at night
Polly put the pickle jar lid on tight
Home before supper
Not past then
Or you'll take a trip with the Gentleman

And by the time they got to the last word, which was "Gentleman," sung in a way that made me know it wasn't the kind of gentleman I'd been familiar with, it became clear that they were looking, singing, directly at me. The mood of their song scared me some, like it was a ghost story told at a sleepover. I wondered what kind of a Gentleman would be so scary that a girl would have to be home before supper.

I stepped closer to them, the whip of the rope cutting inches in front of my chin, fanning my bangs like weeds alongside a highway. Again, I kept walking, and they kept whipping, and soon I was inside the eggbeater arc, jumping, by myself, and there were no more songs being sung. "What's your song mean?" I asked.

"What do you mean, what's it mean?"

"Never heard it before," I said.

"That's because you don't belong here," Sarah said.

"You farm girls sing ne-gro songs," Annie followed.

"Do not," I said, although Charlie and I sang together all the time at the Apple-O.

"Do so."

"Do not."

"Do so."

Do not do so donotdoso.

Still jumping. They whipped faster.

"Make you girls a bet," I said.

"Why?"

" 'Cause I like making bets."

"What's in it for us?" Annie asked.

"You win and I'll never come round you again," I said.

"And if we lose?"

"Just gotta be nice to me and my friend Ed."

"Ed never talks," said Sarah.

"Probably since you'd just be mean to him if he did," I explained.

"Maybe."

"So what's your bet?" Annie asked.

"You follow sports?" I asked.

"No."

"No."

"Uh-uh."

"We're girls!"

"Yeah, okay," I said. "This one's easy anyway. My brother Jerry says that in the next ten years the Chicago Cubs will go undefeated for a whole season."

"What?"

"Your brother's crazy!"

"Still," I say, "he's my brother and I believe him. So, if he's right, meaning that *I'm* right, then you gotta be nice to me. If we're wrong, meaning *I'm* wrong, then you'll never see me again."

"You're going to lose!" Annie said. "Nobody's ever went undefeated, except in high school."

"Still. That's the bet."

"You'll lose."

I said, "Not unless we shake on it. That's what makes the bet official."

And the rope dropped down onto the floor so we could shake, which I made sure to do in plain view of Sister Helen Rose.

Walking down the hallway back into the classroom, Ed ran up beside me and said, "Why'd you bring me into it?"

"Into what?"

"All that! You said they'd have to be nice to me, too, so now they think we're friends. They'll hate me."

"They already do."

Ed hesitated. "They might not."

"Of course they do. Everyone does. I've only been here two days and even *I* know that."

Ed straggled a couple steps behind me. Then caught up again. "Well, anyway, that was the stupidest bet I've ever heard. There's no way you'll win, Plenty."

"Yeah, I know," I said. "But I won't be around in ten years to lose, so what's it matter?" He fell behind again, but I looked back over my shoulder just in time to flash him a smile.

Ed stood still while I kept walking, looking like he was in deep thought, and then he started laughing. He laughed all the way down the hall and all the way into the classroom. He was still laughing when Sister Helen Rose dropped the book she'd held on to during recess right down on my desk and winked.

Ed whispered, "You got your book."

"Sure did," I said.

After school, he waited for me to gather up my things so we could walk out to meet his father together. There was a book in my hand. This was when I knew I had a friend. And being that we were friends, I decided he'd be the best person to ask about a Gentleman.

7.

ED LEFT A lit flashlight on his windowsill, pointed out at the tree that grew outside of his window, the one that was good for climbing.

I waited until it was late at night, until all my brothers and sisters were sleeping. Then I snuck out of the bedroom. I tiptoed down the hall, avoiding those places along the floor that only seemed to creak during the night when I was trying to get out of the house without anyone knowing, and slid down the banister of the stairs, which saved me from any unnecessary thumping.

Ed would be asleep. But he promised to leave the flashlight on his windowsill, promised to leave it there so that the yellow light would create a beam out his window, illuminating the tree outside his room. I would climb the tree and knock on his window and he would tell me about a Gentleman.

I was in the kitchen, where I'd seen Marcie leave her shoes after dinner. I planned on taking her shoes, since mine were in the bedroom and would require too much rustling to get at, and wear them straight across the yard. But when I got to the kitchen, the shoes were nowhere to be found.

I decided to go outside without them, figuring that Mama must have thrown the shoes in our closet while I was brushing my teeth, which was why I did not see her do it. Ed could tell me about a Gentleman just as easily in the morning, but I knew he would probably be disappointed if he woke up to a flashlight with dead batteries and found that I never came.

The ground outside the kitchen was slippery and frozen since we'd only had one snow since October and each day it melted and turned to mud, only to freeze each night and melt again every morning. By now there was hardly a trace of white left, which was why Mama called it the ugliest time of the year. I went to the water pump and ran my hands and feet under the cold water, which was a trick I'd learned about winter. The colder your hands and feet, the less you feel, which makes something like tree climbing in the middle of the night that much easier.

That was when I heard the laughter. It was coming from the area near the barn where the cars were parked. I decided to investigate since this was my house, my yard, and any sort of laughing should be in my awareness.

Father's Dodge was rocking and the windows were steamed up. Inside, I could see that two people were sitting next to each other, holding each other. I thought of Marcie's shoes, the ones that had went missing, and suddenly it occurred to me that maybe Mama didn't put the shoes away after all. Maybe Marcie was entertaining. And being that it was after midnight, and Marcie was only sixteen, and I know the rules about sixteen, and how the rules apply to boys who try to talk to the Porter girls. (Because boys hope for nothing more than baby-making, day in and day out, which was probably true of my brothers, even though I didn't like to think about it. And when I did think of my brothers that way, I also thought about vomiting, or punching them in the chest again and again until their ribs broke, so they'd be bedridden and too sore to wrestle with girls—the ones who were not Porters but for whom the same rules hopefully applied.) For these reasons, and for all the others, I knocked on the window of the Dodge.

Which was when I heard a girl who was not Marcie scream.

"Do you know what time it is?"

"Do *you*?" I asked Bob. We were outside the Dodge, the doors open, the fogged-up windows not so fogged up anymore.

"I'm not a child," Bob said.

"Then why are you living with your folks?" I asked.

This made the girl laugh from inside the cab. Her hair was in a tussle, but her clothes were neatly placed and didn't seem all that wrinkled. Bob looked back at her and shook his head. "Have you ever met my sister, Sharon?" he asked.

"No," Sharon said. "Which one's this?"

"This one's Plenty," I said.

"Sharon—"

"Sharon Stuckly, I know," I said.

"You do?" Bob asked.

"I was with you when you two first started talking," I told Bob. "At the fair, remember? What'd you win, Sharon?"

"A beauty pageant," she said, and I giggled because she wasn't telling the whole truth.

"Be nice, Plenty."

"They gave you that big ole ribbon, I remember. Crowned you—"

"Plenty," Bob said.

Sharon Stuckly had worn a bathing suit in a beauty contest at the fair and pranced around on a stage, while Bob watched from the back of the bleachers, smoking through a pack of cigarettes like they were lemon drops. She was from Monmouth, and was popular because she was seen once at the lake (which really wasn't a lake, because it had been dug up and filled with water by the railroad so that the trains could fill up and make steam on long trips) stripping down to stark nakedness and diving into the water on the night of her high school graduation. She was the kind of girl who would win lots of pageants if she had enough money to travel from fair to fair in order to compete. But because her father was a "degenerate," meaning that he drank and didn't come home at night, Sharon had to settle for the fair in

Monmouth, which was where Bob and me first saw her compete.

At the end of that day, the judges, all men from the Monmouth slaughterhouse, unanimously decided to reward her—as much for her endurance of a father with nasty habits as for her pretty face—and handed her a crown and a ribbon that gave her the honor of being, for the rest of the year, "Miss Teen Prime Beef." This was the title I reminded her of that night, after catching her in the process of steaming up the windows of Father's Dodge with Bob.

"Hey," Sharon mumbled, "It got me a trip to Chicago." But I could tell I'd rattled her some, because she started pulling hairs out from her eyebrows in quick tugs, inspecting them in her fingertips before blowing them into the air.

Bob went around to the other side of the Dodge and told Sharon he'd take her home in just a second but first he needed to talk some to his sister. He shut the door and walked up real close to me, closer than I was used to being with my brothers, and said, "I'm living here because Dad needs the help. Sharon's my girl and you won't talk to her like that if you know what's good for you." I didn't. I'd never known what was good for me. I just did. And then things happened.

Like this. This thing happened. I insulted Sharon for being Miss Teen Prime Beef, which was sort of the same as insulting her for having trash for a father, and Bob forgot all about the fact that I was out of the house in the middle of the night. He forgot about everything except calming Sharon down and taking her home. He got back inside the truck and not long after, I watched it pull quietly out of the yard. There'd be a little time before he'd be back, so I ran over to Ed's house, to the tree just outside his window, and hopped from one foot to the other, like I was standing on coals and not ice, while trying to figure out the best way up the trunk.

The flashlight Ed promised shone down from the window and flowed around the top branches, grazing the edges of the bark. It might have been easier to climb without the light, since it hinted at places to grip that were not nearly as strong as other places might have been. But I was determined to get to the window and to Ed, so I wrapped each leg around the trunk and shimmied up just like I'd seen men from the electric company do when they had to get up high on the poles that lined the easement near the river.

The flashlight glared from behind the glass of the window and made my eyes squint. I could not see into Ed's room, but I was sure Ed could see me, were he awake, were he waiting up and watching. The thought of him watching me when I could not see him made me a bit panicky. I wished I had a flashlight of my own, one that I could shine back through the window, into Ed's room, blinding him just as his flashlight blinded me. Then neither of us would have an advantage over the other, because we'd both be equally unseeable.

But it wasn't the panic of being seen that brought

me down from the tree. Just as I began to knock on Ed's window, about to learn the truth about a Gentleman, Father's voice broke my forward movement. This was why I went back down the tree: I heard Father's voice calling for Marcie! And Plenty! From the front of the house.

Rachel heard the Dodge start up in the middle of the night. She woke up confused, thinking it was morning. When she sat up in bed, she noticed that the bed she shared with both me and Joyce was short one person. It was when she made it to the bedroom door that she noticed that the *other* bed was short one person, too.

She checked the kitchen first and saw that the backdoor was slightly ajar. Cold air seeped in through the crack between the door and the frame, but she did not shut the door then. She moved back up the stairs and went straight into the bedroom to check the closets and see whose things were missing. She saw that my shoes were still there, but Marcie's were gone. About that time, Joyce woke up from the rustling and asked what Rachel was doing. Rachel didn't take the time to explain. She had a funny feeling, which was why she went straight into the boys' room to wake up Bob and Dean.

Dean explained about Bob's date with Sharon Stuckly, and Rachel blushed a little at the thought. Bob was her brother, and Sharon was known to be a loose girl, and no sister should have those images of her brother stuck in her head. Now Dean was out of bed and joining the search, not because he was all that worried, but because Rachel seemed worried, and Rachel was almost like having a second mother, since she was the oldest girl in the house—and girls who could be mothers probably already have some sort of intuition about dangerous things. At least that's what Dean told me the next day, when I asked.

But it was Johnny who found the blood.

When I made it down from the tree and to the front of the house where Mama and Father and everyone else was fanning out into the yard, Mama grabbed me up into her arms and started checking for cuts. "I'm fine," I kept saying, but Mama kept looking, pawing my skin like a cat licking her kitten, until she was sure the blood was not mine. They were asking me where Marcie was, but I didn't know. I tried telling them about Bob and Sharon and the fogged-up windows, but no one would listen. Father ran inside the house and came back with a shotgun. Mama said, "Go inside the house, Plenty."

The upstairs hallway flickered from a lamp burning on the floor of the washroom. The closer I got to the door, the more of the lamp I could see. The sides of the tin tub seemed wet because of the orange light that bounced off its edges. But as I stepped inside, everything made sense—the reason for the yelling and the shotgun in Father's hands. The tin tub was wet, but not with water. The tin tub was wet with blood. There were fingerprints smeared along the inside of the tub, and the floor was peppered with dime-sized spots. Outside they were yelling for Marcie, running down the road in front of our house, passing Mr. Prindergast's place. Which was when I knew they were going the wrong way.

From the window in our bedroom I could see the flashlights, hear the footsteps, but I could not see the people, the Porters, because they were in the front yard, not in the back, where I was looking. They were running down Shanghai Hill. They were moving from one of Jerry's cars to the other, trying to get at least one of them to start. This night, which was like night always was in Alexis—which was black—was also alive in noise: gasping engines, desperate voices. But from the window in the room where I sleep with my sisters, the view is different than the view is from on the ground. The view from that window is only of the cornfields, the backside of the barn, and the trees that line the land that is not our land—the land that is Mr. Prindergast's land. It was dark up and inside those trees that night. The street at the front of the house was full of activity, but the trees behind the fields were dark and still. The limbs had lost their leaves. I don't remember there being a time when they were *losing* their leaves, I remember only a time when there were leaves, and a time when there were not.

This was not the first time I noticed the lack of leaves. They'd been gone since before my twelfth birthday. They'd been gone since I saw Marcie standing under them late at night, at an hour much the same, when she was nothing but a trembling shadow, standing in a grove of trees that had lost all their leaves, just like she had lost her hair.

PART TWO

In which Plenty Porter is put in charge of something important, in more than one way

8.

CHARLIE PLAYED my favorite song on the juke. I'd never heard it before, but from the opening note I knew it would be my favorite.

"What's on your mind, Plenty?" Charlie asked, bringing me over another soda.

"What do you know about Gentlemen, Charlie?" I asked.

Charlie sat down backward on a chair at my table and leaned in. "I know it takes a man to be one."

"Think a Gentleman would ever hurt a little girl?"

"If he did, then he would be no gentleman in my book."

The Apple-O was cold, as usual. The thing about the Apple-O is that it's always the same temperature as it is outside. No matter what you do, there is no way of keeping the cold out or the heat in. The last few days since I found Marcie bleeding out in the trees, I'd been coming to the Apple-O after school to read from the books that I'd been borrowing from

Sister Helen Rose. Mr. Prindergast drove Ed home after school, just like he normally did, and I was supposed to go straight to the hospital, where someone from my family would be with Marcie until after suppertime. I went to the Apple-O instead.

At first Charlie would ask if he should call home and tell my pa where it was that he could find me, but each time he'd ask I'd say, "You can call, but nobody'll be there."

"Where are they?" he'd ask.

"Hospital."

"Shouldn't you be with them if everyone's there?"

"Got too much work to be bothered into stopping by the hospital."

"That so?" he'd ask, like he didn't believe me.

"Well, I'll go over there in a little bit. Just need to finish up a few things first."

But after a few days, Charlie stopped asking any questions. I think he knew deep down the real reason I was staying away from the hospital. Which was that it scared me to see Marcie the way she looked, her arms all stitched up and wrapped in gauze, her head bald, except for the few strands of hair that still flowed from the top of her head, straight on down to her shoulders. I stayed away so that Marcie would never see that thing in my face that shows I'm scared or upset. When Mama looked at Marcie, it was like she was looking at the best version of Marcie, the Marcie who was all dolled up for prom. When I looked at her, I saw the Marcie that was really there. Which somehow wasn't Marcie at all.

The night Marcie was taken to the hospital I was left at Mr. Prindergast's place until morning. I was given a blanket and a pillow and told that the couch was mighty comfortable. Mr. Prindergast went to bed and not long after, Ed came downstairs and sat on the floor next to the couch. It was too dark to see each other, so we did not look. I was on my back, looking up at the ceiling, which might as well have been the night sky. And Ed, sitting on the floor with his back resting against the arm of the couch, looked far into the depths of the house. For a while we did not speak. For a while we spoke about nothing much at all. And then Ed asked if I wanted to hear about a Gentleman.

"There was this girl named Alice," he began. "I never met her, but she went to our school a few years back."

"Was Sister Helen Rose her teacher?" I asked Ed, forgetting for a moment that the only reason Ed and I were talking right now was because Marcie had tried to kill herself. It was as if I were sitting outside on his tree, just after I knocked on the window, just as we had planned all day long.

"No, Sister Helen Rose wasn't teaching back then. I don't know whose class Alice was in."

"Then how'd you hear about her?" I asked, already not sure if I believed him.

"I heard some of the ladies at the feed store talking about her once," he said. "My pa leaves me in there from time to time when he has to do business outside. This one time the ladies forgot I was in there, so I hid inside a closet and listened real close to what they were saying."

"So, what'd they say?"

"I guess this Alice girl liked to write to people who lived far away. She'd go to the library and get addresses out of books and just start sending letters to people she'd never met."

I thought about Far Away and wondered if someone who lived someplace exciting thought that someplace that was not exciting, like Illinois, was Far Away.

One day, Alice got it inside her head that she wanted to live someplace Far Away, and so one day on the way to school, she simply turned left when she should've turned right, and walked clear on out of Illinois.

"Where'd she go?" I asked, turning onto my side to gaze into the part of the house that Ed seemed lost inside.

"That's the thing," he said. "For a long time no one knew. Then one day, a few months later, her mama got a letter in the mail from a place called Idaho. The address was written in Alice's handwriting. Her mama opened the letter, but it was empty."

"Why'd she bother to send an envelope with no letter?" I asked.

"Her mama called the police in Idaho. I guess they thought that Alice sent the envelope as a call for help."

"If she wanted help why didn't she write the word 'help' inside?" I asked.

"That's what I wondered. Anyway, I guess the police

in Idaho never found Alice. The only clue they could find was that there'd been a man who had been seen driving through town in a fancy black car with a little girl inside. Someone at a diner said that they saw the two of them eating breakfast and the little girl called herself Alice."

"It was her!"

"Maybe. No one knows. Anyway, you wanted to know what a Gentleman was. The police told those ladies in the feed store that Alice probably got in the man's car because it was fancy and looked safe. They said that he probably looked and talked like a real Gentleman."

By the time Marcie's arms were stitched up and she was moved from St. Mary's Hospital to that "other" hospital, the one next to St. Mary's, where people went who weren't right in the head, the one with locks on the doors, everyone in town—even Charlie who was colored and owned a juke joint—knew about the thing that had happened inside the Porter house that night. But Charlie never asked about her. Never pressed me for information, which was what I liked about Charlie and the Apple-O. No matter how much he and the people inside the Apple-O knew about me, they never asked. My life outside of the Apple-O was as separate as theirs were to me.

"So you think a girl, or even a boy, I guess, could trust a Gentleman if they needed to?" I asked Charlie.

"Well," he said, getting real thoughtful, "I suppose

if the man was a real gentleman, then yes, I think a girl, or even a boy, could."

Charlie got up from the table while I stayed sitting, wondering how you could tell a real gentleman from a fake Gentleman.

"I think you got company, Plenty," Charlie said when he returned to his rocking chair outside the front door of the Apple-O.

"I don't think so," I said. Who'd come looking for me at the Apple-O when no one knows I visit the O?

"Not too many white boys your age usually dangle behind that tree across the way. Sure he's not waiting for you?"

I found Ed hiding behind a tree, just like Charlie said. He refused to cross the street, not because Charlie was colored and the Apple-O was a place that served alcohol and played music that made hips sway—at least that's what Ed said. He explained that he couldn't cross the street because the sidewalk ends just down from the O, and he was wearing shoes that couldn't get muddy.

"It's okay, Plenty," Charlie said. "You go on and play with your friend."

But it didn't seem right that I left one friend for another, so I stepped into the street, halfway between Charlie and Ed, and introduced the two of them from afar. Charlie waved at Ed and Ed waved back.

"Now you're both acquainted," I said, hoping that made it less rude for me to run off with Ed and leave

Charlie behind. At the very least, Charlie would know he could come with us if he wanted.

"I've been thinking a lot about Alice," I told Ed as we started walking up the sidewalk toward the round-about in the center of Galesburg.

"What about her?"

"I wonder . . ."

"What?" he asked.

"I wonder if she was ever really in danger with that Gentleman."

"Of course she was."

"I'm not so sure. Maybe she sent that letter to her mama, not 'cause she needed help, but just to show her that she was okay. Maybe she met that man in the fancy car and he was taking her someplace good."

"That's not what the police said."

"They missed the biggest clue, though. The biggest clue was the lady who saw Alice and the Gentleman in the diner. She didn't say anything about the girl looking scared or beat up, did she?"

Ed thought about this some. "I don't think so."

"I wonder . . ." I said again. We'd come to the roundabout. It suddenly occurred to me that Ed was with me in Galesburg more than an hour after school got out. "Why aren't you at home, Ed?"

"My daddy said I could stick around."

"To do what?" I asked.

"I dunno." Ed was fumbling inside his pockets, which is something I'd noticed he did when he had something specific on his mind that he was too embarrassed to talk about out loud.

"How are you getting home?" I asked.

"I'll find a ride."

"With who?"

"I guess you. With your folks. If that's all right."

"Well, hell, Ed," I said, "I guess it's going to *have* to be all right, since your daddy already left you here."

I was walking back up the street toward St. Mary's and Ed ran up next to me, breathing all heavy, and said, "You sure?"

The day after the night Marcie became something else, Doc Wander came to visit the house. Mama had left the blood in the washroom, but shut the door so none of us could go inside to see what blood looks like during the day. I wondered how she knew that I was wondering what blood looks like during the day. She showed Doc Wander up to the washroom, and Rachel started to follow after them, because she was a nurse, and what was going on upstairs was medical, but Mama told her to look after her sisters, and I knew she was talking mostly about me.

Father could not sit most of the day. He worked the yard harder than I've ever seen him work. He did not rest. He stacked scraps of wood, moved car parts out from under the hood of Jerry's car, organized paint cans along the shelves in the barn. Mama called from the back door that it was time to come inside because Doc Wander was here. When Father came inside, he was damp with sweat, but still he did not sit. None of us did. Doc Wander sat alone on the couch, in front of the fire, and began to tell us about Marcie's hair. "It will grow back if she lets it grow back."

"How can *she* do that, Doc? Hair just grows," I said.

"Shut up, Plenty," Rachel said.

"It's a good question," Father said.

"There's no way of telling why she lost her hair," Doc Wander said. "There's no telling until she tells us. If it was some sort of trauma, or if it's guilt, or depression, none of that really matters. She's going to have to remember how to do things, all over again. But whatever it is that has kept her from growing hair, well, my bet is that same thing caused her to do what she did. And being that no one here knew what was going on with Marcie, she must be really good at keeping things to herself. There's twelve other people in this house, and not one of you knew a thing. We have a lot of work to do. And it's going to take time."

"And money," Father said.

On the way out to his car, I stopped Doc Wander. I told Mama I wanted to wish him luck with my sister, but really I wanted to confess. He lifted my chin with his finger and asked, "Why are you crying?"

"I knew about Marcie's hair," I said. "She told me and I kept it a secret."

"Have you told anyone? Your mama, maybe, or one of your sisters?"

"No, sir. I wish I would've. But I didn't." And I was sobbing even harder.

But then Doc Wander had an idea. He bent down in front of me and said, "Keep your secret. Marcie knows she can trust you because you never gave her secret away. Maybe she'll keep telling you things. Maybe not right away, but over time. You might be the one who could put the pieces together."

"And help Marcie remember how to grow her hair back?" I asked, as if I'd been put in charge of something important.

"Maybe so."

Three weeks later I had still not stepped foot into Marcie's room alone. I knew I would have to eventually—especially since I went to school right down the street from her hospital and could get there on recess if I wanted, but I didn't know what to say to her. And, maybe even worse, I didn't know what it was she might say to me.

I brought Ed with me to the hospital the afternoon he met me at the Apple-O, only because Ed needed a ride home. But by the time we got to her room, I was glad he was there. Mama met us in the hallway and sat us down with Marcie's nurse—a "lovely woman named Sally," she said. I laughed when Ed shook Sally's hand. Sally and Charlie shared the same color.

"Stick around me," I told Ed, "and you'll be meeting all sorts of people I bet you never would have met."

"What makes you think I want to stick around you?" he asked.

"Of course you do, Ed. Who else you got?"

Ed got real quiet then. At first I thought it was because of what I said; maybe it reminded him of his mother. But then I realized he got quiet because the door to Marcie's room had opened. And he could see directly inside. He could see Marcie in bed, see her hands tied to the bedposts with plastic, could see her mouth drooping, as if she was sleeping, although her eyes were wide open. Mama came to the door, smiling as if nothing was abnormal inside that room. She said, "Come on inside and say hello, you two. She's just waking up."

I went to sleep that night thinking about Alice. It made sense to me that she would have left. What other choice did she have? Stick around something hard and you lose your hair. Then you become something of a mystery that people are scared of. It made sense to me why men like Charlie had to live separate from the rest of us, own their own bars, live near the river in a community of outsiders, why my grandpa would disappear and never talk to any of us again. But the thought of hiding like I do in the forts I build between our two beds for the rest of my life seemed terrible. Head for the road and you get roadside meals with fancy strangers. Ed had missed the point of her letter. That girl Alice got to step out of herself and take a ride with a Gentleman—a ride that took her as far as Idaho, and probably much, much farther.

Someday, I thought, Alice might find herself shaking hands with another girl her age. They'd get to talking about places they'd been, where they came from, old friends, and the name of St. Joseph's Middle School would pass over both their lips. Then they'd laugh at the coincidence of two girls who'd went to the same school back when they were children, who'd found the company of a Gentleman, and with it, the openness of places outside of their homes. Upon meeting, one of them would say, "We're lucky, you and me, Alice," and the other would reply, "We are, Plenty. We are."

9.

THE FIRST TIME I visited Marcie alone in the hospital.

10.

THE NEXT TIME I was going to visit, I wrote out what it was that I wanted to say on a sheet of paper that I borrowed from Ed after school.

"Are you going to give it back?" he asked.

"What?"

"The piece of paper?"

"Why would I do that?" I asked.

"You said you were going to borrow it. So I'm wondering when I'm going to get it back."

"You ain't never gonna get it back."

"There you go again!" he hollered.

"What?"

"A double negative."

"Okay," I said, learning as I went, "you *are not* going to get it back."

"Why are you borrowing it, then?"

"I'm not! I'm *taking* it!" I said.

"Then that's what you should have said to begin with."

I told him that I was going to *take* a piece of paper, that I would not give it back, that the paper would be soiled with my words, words that would be written out on the piece of paper—the one that I would *take* and not *borrow*, and those words, the ones written, the ones that I wrote, would be recited like a poem or a prayer to my sister Marcie, and that, mostly, I hoped those words, the ones written on the page that I *took*, that when I said them, when I read them aloud like a poem or a prayer, that maybe they would get her to talk some when I visited. Because the last time, which was the day before, I sat next to her on the bed for over an hour and neither of us said nothing.

"Anything," Ed corrected. "Neither of you said *anything*."

Which was true.

II.

HERE ARE SOME *things that I want to remember: I hated you for not listening when I tried to tell you about the watch that I found, the one that belonged to Mr. Prindergast.*

I don't hate you anymore because now Mr. Prindergast takes me to school with his boy, Ed. Our teacher, Sister Helen Rose, let me read a book last week, my first book, so now I am glad that he got his watch back.

The first time you showed me you lost some of your hair I wanted to tell Mama right away because it scared me.

"Do we have to do this, Plenty?" Marcie asked.

"Do what?"

"Talk about this stuff. You can just sit there. That's fine with me—we don't have to talk."

"Well," I said. "We're not really talking. It's more like I'm reading something that I wrote than talking."

"But you're reading *to* me."

"What else do you have to do? You got a boy coming over? A hot date?" I didn't laugh at the joke, even though I was the one who made it. Marcie looked out the window at her left. It looked out on a tree, one branch of a tree, nothing else.

The first time you showed me you lost your hair I wanted to tell Mama right away because it scared me. It scared me a lot. I didn't tell her, because we made a promise, you and me. I kept the promise. Still have. No one knows what you showed me that morning, the morning just after I turned twelve.

Last night, I pulled on a clump of my hair as hard as I could so that I'd lose my hair, too. Not much of it came out. It hurt real bad and when I touched the place on my scalp where the hair sticks into the skull, the place I tried to rip it from, it was wet. I thought there would be blood on my fingers, but it wasn't blood. It was this clear, watery liquid, but thicker than water, like sugar water. When I woke up this morning I could feel a scab.

I wonder if it hurts when your hair falls out. Or if it did at one time.

"It doesn't. It never did."

"Oh," I said. "Okay."

Some other things I remember:

That time Jerry got onto the handlebars of Rachel's bike and the two of them went riding down Shanghai Hill and they hit a bump—

"And Jerry's foot got stuck in the spokes—" Marcie added.

"And he almost cut his heel off," I finished, and waited for Marcie to turn back toward me. But she didn't. We stayed quiet for a time.

"What else do you have written there?" she asked.

"Well—"

There was that winter, a couple years ago, when Johnny almost burnt the firehouse down, the one on Losey Street, 'cause he was going to start a fire outside to keep us all warm, but used gasoline to do it. The fire spread through all the scrub brush and started to climb up the firehouse.

"No, something else," Marcie said.

"What?"

"Tell me something else."

"Like what."

"I don't know. Something about you."

"Me?"

"Something embarrassing," Marcie said, and scratched her head. "Anything embarrassing in there?"

And there was.

When I was little, Mama walked by me once when I was crying. I'm not sure why I want to remember this, but sometimes when I have nothing else to think about I make myself remember what happened. I was on the porch. I remember that much, being on the porch, but not much before. I remember that one of the boys hurt my feelings because they were cussing on a Sunday—that was it, he was cussing on a Sunday, and I thought for sure he was going to go to Hell on Judgment Day, and it made me real upset. Mama came up to the porch from the yard and saw me sitting there, just sitting there on the porch with my knees drawn up to my chin, and I was crying. Sobbing. I guess she could see pretty easily that I wasn't hurt, wasn't bleeding or nothing, but it didn't really matter, did it? I was a little girl, I was her little girl, and I was crying, and she walked right past me. Didn't say a thing. She just took a step around me and went on inside the house.

"Mama doesn't do well with crying."

"What?" I asked, sniffling some.

"It makes her nervous."

"How do you know?"

"She told me once. When I was your age."

"What'd she say?" I asked.

"I dunno. She just said. I might've been crying myself—probably was. Anyway. I dunno, she sat down and told me that she doesn't like to hear crying. It makes her nervous."

"Why would someone's crying make her nervous? That doesn't make no sense."

"Makes sense to me," Marcie said, and looked to the left. "She probably feels like she's supposed to do something to make everything better but doesn't know what to do."

"How hard is it to rub someone's back?"

"Who'd she have to rub her back when she was little and crying? Her mother was dead. Her daddy was a drunk. Still is to this day, and you know it. He went off to live near the mill and now everyone in town laughs at her. If she cried, no one would ever have noticed. Especially her daddy, because he was gone. So she probably just learned not to cry."

I thought about that some. "You can learn not to cry?"

Marcie thought about that some, too. She thought about it for a long while. So long that I almost turned away, to the window where there was a tree branch and no trunk. Then she answered. She said, "Yes, you can learn not to cry."

I knew we weren't talking about the same thing anymore.

12.

SADIE DIED two days before Christmas. Sadie was my chicken.

She didn't come to the fence for her morning feeding, so I climbed into the pen and found her near the barn, lying on her side with one stiff wing stretched upward, casting a bit of shade over her face. Father came running from the field when he heard me screaming. All I could say was, *"Sadie."* Over and over again, *"Sadie. Sadie. My Sadie."* Father looked up at the sky and the clouds in the sky for a long time, almost as if he were not used to such things. I waited for his eyes to return to the ground, to me, but for some time they did not. I myself did not look up at the sky then. The sky had nothing to do with taking my Sadie away from me.

I was sobbing when he told me "Everything is still up there, Plenty—the sky is gray and the clouds are black." I told him I didn't need telling what I could easily see for myself. He squatted next to me and ripped a handful of icy weeds from the ground. They chattered inside his palm like dice. He told me that God takes a deep breath before a storm and that's what caused the cold and the ice on the grass. And that was why Sadie died. "Sometimes cold can come like a snap, and if you're caught standing outside in that one moment, you'd see the whole sky ice over and crack in an instant," he said. "Sadie died because she saw God's very breath, Plenty, and there's not much point in living after seeing something as wonderful as that."

Father took Sadie from my hands and carried her inside the house where Mama was scrubbing dishes. She asked about the eggs, but Father said it was too late; they'd been out in the freeze for too long a time. The chicks would never hatch. "It's going to blizzard," he told Mama. "There won't be traveling on Christmas." Mama went to the window and sighed in a way that meant, "Oh, no."

They were thinking of Marcie being alone in the hospital on the day Jesus was born, while I was thinking about chickens and the eggs that would not hatch because there was no longer a Sadie to sit on them. God took a breath and Sadie died. First I thought God had proven Himself indifferent to all us Porters—which was a word I'd learned from Debbie just last week after witnessing Ronnie Taylor point into the bleachers at Patricia Johnson after he scored the winning basket against Monmouth High. ("I don't care who Ronnie Taylor does or does not point at in the bleachers,"

Debbie said. "I'm *indifferent* to the boy.") What kind of God, other than an indifferent one, would take away a family's chicken without first giving a little life to her chicks? But then I started thinking that maybe those chicks were even luckier than Sadie. They got to see Heaven before ever having to deal with Illinois.

"No, *I* better stay with Marcie in the hospital," Father was saying. Mama was getting things ready to pluck feathers from Sadie's body. Just like that, my pet was becoming dinner. But this was nothing new to me. I'd stopped crying and demanding funerals and eulogies years ago. Mama used to point to the sky and say that all my animals, even the ones we ate, were high up in Heaven watching over us with a giggle. I wondered where the sky ends and Heaven begins. I used to think that maybe the sky was really just the underside of Heaven's floor, but that, too, stopped making sense. How could a place that can't be seen exist? And how could someone, like Sadie and her chicks, live there?

"We can go see Marcie together today before the storm starts up strong," Father continued. "And then I'll stay on with her through Christmas." Mama was about to put up a fuss, but Ed came to the door and started knocking with both fists like he was collecting money for the bank, or his father, or both.

"We can see you through the window, Ed," I said, and opened up the door. He flew right by me like I was nothing but a ghost and went straight to Mama's side, watching as she bound Sadie's feet with string.

"Sadie died . . . of natural causes," I told the back of his head.

Ed was practically clinging to the hem of Mama's skirt. "That right, Mrs. Porter?" he asked. "You gonna fix her for Christmas supper?"

Mama snapped up a rag and told me to take Ed outside to the pump to fill up a pot with water, which really meant that she wanted us out of her hair.

"C'mon, Ed," I said, dragging him from the kitchen. I heard Father saying he didn't like the idea of *Mama* sitting alone in that hospital for two or three days with Marcie while the blizzard kept us all apart, but that's all I gathered, because the door had swung shut behind us.

Ed hopped down the steps on both feet and walked out into the yard. He tried to whistle but spit by accident. Then he took off running. And before I knew it, I took off after him, and we were running, the both of us, racing each other to the pump, our feet slipping on the fresh ice that blanketed the yard. He was about to beat me, and I found myself wishing it would start to blizzard so that no one would see me lose to a Prindergast. A few strides later, our lungs were burning from the thin, cold air. We gave up the race without discussion and walked the rest of the way.

By the time we reached the pump, we were panting so hard that it took the two of us to get the iron arm to budge. Our fingers were bright pink. Ed switched hands every couple pumps to shake out the free one, as if it burned. I licked a bit of snot from my upper lip. Water was pouring out of the spout and into the pot, and I watched ice crystals tumble in the froth. I did not tell Ed about the crystals, even though it would have been something to talk about. I wasn't used to being out with Ed in the yard, because Ed never seemed the type for getting his trousers dirty, and besides, if he was, I always had the feeling that his pa didn't like him crossing to our side of the road. "So . . ." I said, and watched the word dangle between us in a cloud of our breath.

"Can't wait for Christmas," he blurted, a little too loud. His voice had the abrupt sound of a thought trapped inside his head for too long a time. "Can you?"

"Haven't been excited for Christmas since I was five," I said, and then sneezed.

"Your mom's gonna fix up a big dinner, I bet."

"*Jesus*! What is it with you and my mom all of a sudden?" I asked, walking to the house, trying to steady the heavy pot and keep water from sloshing over the sides.

"I was just askin'—" he started.

"Going on and on about her like you about to propose!" I said.

He took up a stutter like a dog that got his leg caught in a barbed-wire fence. Mama heard us on the steps and came to the door. Ed looked up at her, then back at me, all the while still stuttering.

"Ed?" Mama asked. But before she got any sort of answer, he ran off across the road, straight to his house. For a second I thought maybe he was going to cry, but lost track of the idea when I went inside and felt the heat from the stove scorch my chapped cheeks.

"What's wrong with Ed?" Mama asked. As she took the pot and set it over the fire to boil, she said, "He seemed upset."

"Who knows anymore with that boy," I said. "He *perplexes* me!"

"Does he?" Mama asked, amused. I stuck out my arms and warmed my hands a few inches from the stove. The kitchen table was covered with a half-dozen packages neatly wrapped in old newspaper, the print muddied into a yellow smudge. Mama was in the process of wrapping each one with strips of red ribbon that, even though it was wrinkled and frayed, when tied into a bow, it became the caretaker to something secret and important inside. It turned out that I *was* excited for Christmas, and sort of wished I would've told Ed so.

"Where is everyone?" I asked.

"Upstairs getting bundled. You better hurry on up there yourself. We're leaving in a half hour." I knew this meant there'd been a winner to her argument with Father, but by her mood, which was hurried, and yet not quite sulky, I couldn't tell who.

"We going to see Marcie, then?" I asked. Mama dropped her chin into some sort of a nod and checked the pot for signs of a boil. I asked, "Is that what the presents are for?"

"Mm-hmm. "

"We gonna leave 'em there for her?"

"Nope," she said.

"You gonna stay with her till Christmas?"

"You keep wasting all this time by asking questions, you're going to end up getting left behind on Christmas Day."

"There ain't going to be no traveling this year on Christmas," I said, repeating what Father had said.

"This year there will be; we're leaving in a half hour, like I told you."

"That don't make no sense," I said. "Christmas's two days from now."

"Not this year," Mama said, and dropped Sadie into the boiling hot water. "This year Christmas is today."

After lunch, we drove into town. Father seemed to take extra care to drive slowly, as the ice on the road had not yet melted because the sun was caught behind thin clouds. I watched the spirit of our truck following alongside us, and tried to forget that it was only a reflection against the frozen snow. I wished Marcie could've seen the road that afternoon. She always liked the outdoors more than most of us and would've listened when I said that the snow was just as bright as the sky, and probably would have helped me identify the color. But as it were, no one listened, and I squinted into the glare the sunlight made as it pushed through the clouds. It spread thick across the sky, meeting the ground in a brilliant clash of color which I named both white *and* blue, even though I figured there were more colors hidden inside.

And as I thought about things like that, like the number of colors that make up a glare, colors that are both seen and unseen, Heaven started to make more sense to me. Maybe Heaven was as indescribable as a glare, everything and nothing both at once. And then I knew that Sadie and her chicks were okay. They were the stuff that light is made of.

Nurse Sally greeted us with a big grin. It must have been quite an unexpected sight: twelve Porters coming up the stairs, two days before Christmas, each carrying a package wrapped with red ribbon. Father held a grocery sack containing a clean shirt, a book, and his glasses, all folded neatly inside, which I knew meant that he was planning on staying until the end of the storm. Sally clapped her hands together and howled with laughter. "Well, well, well," she said, "isn't this special! We weren't expecting y'all! Your Marcie is truly blessed, I say. Two sets of visitors in one single day!"

Mama frowned a bit and asked what Sally meant. "Who else had come visiting?" The fact was that no one but our family knew Marcie was in the hospital; Marcie didn't want any of her friends from school coming to the mental hospital with fresh-cut flowers, hand-drawn cards with "Get Well Soon" wishes, and surprised, disturbed expressions on their faces after finding their friend, bald and crazy, smiling back at them.

Sally answered, "Why, her granddaddy, of course.

He comes by every couple days and keeps your little one company. Yes, ma'am, Marcie is blessed with family in large quantities!" Sally was laughing again and squeezed past Mama, heading back to her station.

Mama's mouth was twitching, her chin becoming wrinkled as a prune. "Ray," she said to Father, but he squeezed her hand and whispered something into her ear that caused her to nod and relax. Father told us to go on ahead and say hiya to Marcie while he squared away some things with Sally about his staying on through Christmas. Mama nodded again, as if he were talking more to her than to us, and then started walking toward Marcie's room.

Dean and Bob sidled up on both sides of her. "Mama?" Dean asked.

But before he got out another word she said, "Don't say anything. We're here to see Marcie, you hear? Don't say anything more about it, none of you."

And no one did. Including me. We filed into Marcie's small hospital room and played like it was Christmas morning. Marcie wrapped her neck with a natural brown scarf that Martha had knitted from lamb's wool. Against Marcie's pale and sunken skin, the scarf looked like braided hair, and all any of us could think about was how much hair was missing on top of her head. Later, Martha would say she wished she would've chosen a different color, something bright, and knitted with a tighter stitch. But Mama told her that Marcie looked beautiful, and something in her voice made us believe it, too.

Not long after we arrived, the room became dim and tired as the sun set outside. Father said it was best if we got home before it started snowing. Dean took the keys, promising to drive slow and not scare Mother like he sometimes tended to do.

Everyone said their good-byes to Marcie and waited in the hallway while Mama sat on the bed and said something soft. A bit later, she emerged with red cheeks. Father patted her shoulder and said he'd see us all after the storm. Minutes later, we were driving away in the truck, the windows rolled down an inch to keep the windshield from fogging, huddled together for warmth. Mama didn't say much of anything. I thought about asking if she was sad, if she was missing Marcie, or if she was thinking about her pa and was mad that he'd visited Marcie without asking, without ever coming to visit her first. But no question seemed right. I ended up settling on something safer, and asked if we'd still have Christmas on its proper day.

Bob said, "Shut your mouth, Plenty."

I didn't put up a fight. I knew it was a stupid thing to ask. In the quiet, I stuck a finger outside through the space between the window and the door, and felt the first flake of snow drop from the sky and melt instantly against my skin.

13.

AND THEN SOMETHING like a miracle happened. The day before Jesus was to celebrate his birthday, the first of Sadie's chicks hatched.

It was unexpected and thrilling to everyone, me most of all, but what we did not know then was that the very event, something as small and forgettable as seven baby chickens unexpectedly pecking through a thin shell and into a blizzard, would later spark a series of events that would greatly change all of our lives, the lives of the Porters, forever. And I didn't know that the very event would spark something within myself, Plenty Porter, who is both small and forgettable, a curiosity that would place me in the center of those events.

It started with a discussion about heat. The fact that our house is heated by a furnace, and that from the furnace several ducts snake through the walls, up and up, into three separate rooms. And that those ducts are connected to rusted vents in the floor, and that heat spills through those vents, into the three separate rooms in which we sleep in groups—boys, girls, and parents—made it necessary that we would accommodate Sadie's chicks in one of those heated rooms. I demanded that it would be our room they slept in, the room of the girls, not because chicks are better suited with females, but because Sadie was my chicken, and that sort of made me responsible for her kin.

Dean and Jerry filled a box with torn and crumpled newspaper, and took it outside to gather the chicks— which continued to miraculously hatch throughout the day—while the rest of us cleared the room of anything that they could get into and ruin. I thought we should gather up a blanket like a nest on top of the bed and let them have a comfortable mattress on which to sleep. But Rachel said no one would want to sleep on top of bird crap. Which was probably true.

Jerry came up the stairs with the box, shaking flakes of white snow from his hair. I couldn't hear any chirping and asked if the chicks were dead.

"No," Jerry said. "They're alive, just cold." He took them inside the bedroom, and each of us followed. Someone shut the door to keep the heat inside. Jerry set the box on the floor and Mama folded a warm towel on top of them. Their little heads bucked up against the cloth a few times before settling into sleep. Rachel opened the door and, one by one, everyone slipped back into the hallway. There was nothing left to see. I remained sitting on the floor, my back propped against the bed.

"Are you going to stay in here?" Mama asked. I told her I would let her know when the chicks woke up, and she said we could feed them a little something when they did.

Not long after Mama left, I fell asleep.

It was night when I woke to the sound of chirping. Someone had put me inside the bed and pulled the covers up to my chin. My mouth was dry from the heat of the furnace, the sheets damp with sweat. I kicked off the covers and slid to the foot of the bed. Inside the box, the baby chicks were lying together on top of a towel, their heads resting on each other's backs. I wondered how long I'd slept. Thinking it might almost be morning, my heart began racing to thoughts of Christmas.

The front door slammed shut downstairs. I went to the window and saw Mama outside on the porch, bundled in Father's coat and cap. It was deep into night, no signs of morning. Bob came outside after her, and the two of them seemed to have some sort of an argument. After a short exchange, Mama took Bob by the hand, turned him back around, and led him to the door. He said one more thing, waved his arms, and went back inside. I watched from behind the curtain as Mama stuffed her hands inside her pockets and started walking out to the road.

I was careful not to wake any of my sisters as I crept out of the bedroom, passing the chicks on the floor. Bob was in the entryway, putting on a coat of his own, when I peeked over the railing. He was in a hurry, his fingers fumbling with each button, and I knew he was going to follow after Mama. I had no idea how late it was, but since everyone else was sleeping, I figured it was after midnight.

There wouldn't be time for both boots and a coat if I planned on following Bob, so I settled on the boots and pulled open the door. Bob had disappeared into the heavy snowfall but I found him again when he made it to the mailbox, just at the head of the road. He seemed to know exactly where Mama was going. He drew his shoulders up to his ears and hunkered down the road through the snow.

It was much colder than I expected, having been holed up inside the upstairs bedroom all afternoon, and the shock of it made me dizzy. There was no moon in the sky and the farther I moved away from our house, the harder it was to see. I marched to the drumming of my teeth. Each snowflake felt like broken glass cutting into my face. I tried to hold my chin down but found it hard to keep an eye on Bob. I began to get scared of losing him, and myself, out there in the cold.

Maybe it was a bad idea to leave the house, to follow after two people who probably didn't want to be followed. But it was too late for thinking, so I focused on Bob's footprints in the fresh snow. I took two steps for each one of his, and the order of this, two to his one, kept my mind busy until the snow came down too hard and too fast and there were no longer any tracks to follow. I decided to keep walking straight and keep my hopes on running into him somewhere down the road.

By the time I came to the river, which meant I'd long ago gotten off the road, Bob was nowhere to be found. But it didn't matter, because I knew that the river moved west through the cedar trees and eventually ran into a lake that would surely be frozen this time of year. I'd been there once before.

On the edge of the lake there was a small community of log cabins next to the mill, which was where Charlie and the coloreds lived. Figuring that Mama would have no reason to go visit Charlie this late at night, especially since she did not know Charlie in the first place, I began thinking about the tenant house that was built just at the mouth of the river, the one in which my mother had been born. Inside that tenant house lived a father to my mother, and a grandfather to me. By losing track of Bob, and by finding the river, everything became clear—the who, what, where, when, and why of it all, like the makings of a good story. In an instant, I knew exactly where my mother was going, and why my brother would follow her there.

I came into the clearing and heard Mama yelling. She was in the front of the old tenant house, yelling, stumbling backward as Bob held her by the arm. She was flinging words and kicking snow toward the porch. An old man, my grandfather, I guessed, stood in the doorway, eclipsed by the warm light from inside. It had been three years since I'd seen him, and yet I'd never seen him. He was a man who lived in a house that we did not visit, a man we passed on the street in Galesburg one day and did not address. He was coming from an old car, filling his arms with stacks of wood he planned to sell in town. His charms whispered out of earshot by my brothers: *That is your grandfather; he is not a good man. Look at his worn and tired face and don't ever let it be your own.*

Bob pulled Mama away from the river, back into the trees, and I could hardly see them there. I took a step farther into the clearing and realized that they were gone. Mama's voice was a howl from deep within the woods, or maybe it was a coyote. I walked farther into the clearing and thought Grandpa must've seen me, because he took a step down from the porch toward the place where I stood and looked out at the river. I lifted my arm to wave. But then he bent down and picked something up from the snow. I took another step, daring myself to make a sound. But he turned round and walked back to the porch, stomping inside the house with an object hidden in his hand.

Mama and Bob were gone. Grandpa shut the door.

I swayed in the middle of the clearing. My face was burning. I could hear Sadie's chicks chirping inside my head, a desperate sound that caused me to look down. Their box was resting in the snow, at my feet, and while I knew there was no way the box could have followed me there, I did not question the fact that it was there, nonetheless. And in the second before I lost consciousness and fell to the ground, just before everything went dark around me, I watched the seven chicks, huddled helplessly together inside the box that was really not there, use their tiny beaks to peck at each flake of snow, as if to break them apart and stop the sky from falling.

14.

ARE YOU the one who lost her hair?" Grandpa asked, putting another log on the fire.

"That's Marcie," I said, and sat up. A feather puffed out from a hole in the pillow and settled on my shoulder.

"Which one are you, then?" he asked.

Being that this was the first conversation I'd ever had with my mother's father, I felt the need to impress him with my confidence. "I'm Plenty," I said, and tried to remember how it was I got inside his house.

"I bet you are," he said, grinning.

There was a puddle of melted snow on the floor next to my boots, which I located not on my feet, but by the door. The room felt hot, and I thought about asking him to put fewer logs on the fire, but figured Mama would think it rude to make demands in a stranger's home. "Excuse me, sir," I said, "but how long have I been here?"

"All night long, sleeping," he said, removing a red-hot poker from the fire. "And it's not sir you should be calling me."

"Yes, sir, Grandpa," I said, and hoped that he would be pleased.

"Not sure that works, either," he said. "Better if you call me Mr. Darcey, I think."

"Yes, sir, Mr. Darcey."

He left the room and came back with a tattered quilt, and tossed it over my legs. There were so many things about Mr. Darcey and his home that were unexpected. He had a funny way of speaking, which I took to him being from Ireland. He was a tall man, not hunched and beaten, as everyone made him sound. Everything about him was exaggerated—the length of his nose, the shape of his ears, the redness of his skin, like a cartoon in the funny papers. His home was well kept for a man living by himself with no wife to keep after him about things. The dining table was polished and dusted. Four lanterns, globes clean of soot, were hung in each corner of the room. He kept a small stack of wood next to the stove and took care to sweep up any stray splinters before settling across from me in his chair. He picked up a book from the side table and stretched his arm far away from his face, squinting in order to read the print. I asked if I could fetch his glasses so he wouldn't have to get up out of his chair again. But without looking up from his book, he said that he didn't have any glasses and never did. I felt my cheeks getting warm again, this time from shame: I should've known that a man who lived inside a shack, without any animals or crops to his name, couldn't afford spectacles.

"I'm sorry, Mr. Darcey, I didn't mean to—"

Mr. Darcey chuckled, and I knew I hadn't made an offense. His lips made a popping sound as they moved along with the words he read.

"'Scuse me, Mr. Darcey," I swallowed and said, "but what are you planning on doing with me?"

"You came to me all on your own, if you remember. I should be asking what it was you were planning when you decided to pass out in the middle of my yard," he said harshly.

"I wasn't planning nothing, really," I said. "I just wanted to know where Mama was going so late at night."

"Well," he said. "I figure you can get yourself warm and then walk on home, the way you came, and ask her yourself."

I felt myself becoming sad, which he must've noticed, which was something I hated about myself. It was always so easy for folks to tell exactly what I was feeling without me saying a thing.

"What is it?" he asked.

I was afraid I'd cry if I tried to speak, so I shook my head back and forth a couple times, instead.

"What is it?" he asked again.

"Just thought you might want to get to know me some," I said. "Being that we've never met, and all." I doubted that a man who lived alone in the woods with only a few colored people for company would care about such a thing as his eleventh grandkid, but it was my hoping to be wrong that made me say it.

"I'm sorry," he said, and went back to his book.

Then I started to cry, for many reasons, too many to name them all. There was the cold, there was Mama, and Marcie, and the baby chicks, and Mr. Darcey, who was my grandpa, but didn't seem to want to be. There was so much sadness, circling all around me, all the time, and the thought of it, of all those unhappy people, myself included, made my chest hurt so bad, I had trouble breathing. The only one of us who'd had luck of any kind was Sadie. I was jealous, right then, of Sadie, and wished it'd been me out there in the cold two nights ago, me who'd seen God's breath. She'd spent the whole of her life laying eggs out in an ugly barn, and was rewarded by seeing something wonderful and final, like a period at the end of the last sentence in the first book you ever read.

It occurred to me, as I gathered my boots, that maybe some things are worth waiting for, and wondered what it was Mr. Darcey was waiting to see before he died. He'd lived alone all these years, visited by no family, kept company by books. He busied himself with tidying, and yet, had a secret: He'd been visiting Marcie at the hospital. What was he after? Moving away from the door, I set the boots back in the puddle of melted snow on the floor and sat down once again in front of the fire. Mr. Darcey looked up from his book, his eyes squinting, this time toward me, and asked, "What are you doing?"

"I'm staying," I said, folding my arms in a show of stubbornness that drove Mama crazy.

"What for?" he asked.

I looked over my shoulder, out the window, and noticed small details on his porch I hadn't seen the night before, like warped shingles, broken icicles, sights made possible by daylight peeking out from behind the clouds. Mr. Darcey set his book down hard on the side table; the slam reminded me of his question. "It's Christmas," I said.

He leaned back in his chair and thought about it for a long time. A moment later, he wiped his mouth, and said, "So it is."

Over breakfast, he would tell me about Ireland. He was a boy of eight when his daddy couldn't grow anymore potatoes. I guess a lot of people had trouble with potatoes back then. So much trouble, they had to get on a boat and travel for months, across the sea to America. "People were sick on that boat," he told me, "dying from fever," and his mother had to hold him in her arms, the whole trip, to make sure he never got too cold. But by the time they got to some island outside of New York City, she was sick herself, and they wouldn't let her leave. "She died there," Mr. Darcey told me. "In a cramped room, on an island less than two miles from a shore she'd never get to step foot on. She died, alone."

"I guess there was no one there to keep her warm. That reminds me of Sadie," I said.

"Who?" Mr. Darcey said.

"She was my favorite chicken," I said bravely. It didn't seem right to talk about sad things on Christmas, but then I thought about her chicks, and figured Mr. Darcey would like to hear about a miracle. "She died because she saw God's breath. We thought none of her eggs would hatch, since it was so cold out and no one was there to keep them warm." Mr. Darcey frowned, and I continued, "But then a miracle happened, Mr. Darcey. They hatched!" Maybe I was talking too fast because he didn't seem to understand. "Bob says it's a gift from God."

"Be careful," Mr. Darcey said. "I don't want to bawl you out, but my experience is that there are no such things as 'gifts.' What might look like a 'gift' at first can turn on you like the Devil."

We were in the kitchen; he was soaping dishes. He took to a pan with a spatula, scraping bacon grease into a tin cup on the sink. I noticed a cabinet filled to the brim with bottles. I wondered if they were the Devil he was talking about.

"You like my sister Marcie, then?" I asked.

Mr. Darcey set the pan into a sink full of scummy water and left it to soak. He ran his finger along the surface of the water, skating over soap scum like ice. "Like I told your mother, I never met your sister."

"Sure you have, Mr. Darcey," I said. "You've been visiting her every couple'a days, Sally told us."

"Then Sally's a damn liar!" he snapped, and left me in the kitchen alone. I found him standing out on the porch in his shirtsleeves. He wasn't shivering. His arms hung loose at his sides. I walked over and stood next to him and wiggled my toes to keep the rest of me from shaking. I didn't notice then that it had stopped snowing, because Mr. Darcey started talking again about Ireland. He said, "When we first moved into this house, my daddy said the hillside was as close as we'd ever come to seeing Ireland again. He told me, 'Boy-o, whenever you forget your way, just look on at that grass and remember home.'"

"Does it work?" I asked.

Mr. Darcey shook his head. "Would've been different. If we'd stayed there. For us all. Life would've been different for us all."

"No telling," I said, and took his hand.

Mr. Darcey told me to take Pole Line Road through the easement and follow the electric lines all the way into Alexis. "It shouldn't take you more than an hour," he said. "There's probably a faster way, but that's the easiest."

Mama was probably worried sick about me. I'd already missed most of Christmas. There was still time to make it home before it started snowing again, so I wished Mr. Darcey a happy Christmas one more time and climbed down the steps. Just as I passed the place in the snow where I fell the night before, Mr. Darcey called out, "Hey, you forgot something!" I ran back to the porch and asked "What?" He handed me a knit cap, Father's knit cap, the one Mama had been wearing. She must have dropped it. "It'll keep your ears warm," he said, and helped me pull it over my head. "That'll do," he said. "Be sure to give it back to your mama when you get home."

"But—" I started to say, and stopped. If I wore the cap home and gave it to Mama, then she'd know *where* I'd been all day, and *who* I'd been with. But Mr. Darcey knew what I meant. It didn't need saying. He wanted her to know I'd been there, with him. I understood. Without saying another word, I left the porch. By the time I looked back, he'd already shut the door.

I found Pole Line Road without any trouble and slowed my walking some. The wind was blowing, which gave me a shiver, but the trees made music like a wind chime, and I was content with taking my time, despite the cold. There were lots of things to think about, like why Mr. Darcey didn't give me Father's cap when I first tried to leave in the morning. Maybe he knew all along that I'd end up staying. And why hadn't I been nicer to Ed? He was all alone without his mother, just like Sadie's chicks. Maybe he'd like to come over for Christmas dinner—I'd have to remember to ask Mama if it was okay. And hopefully Father would stay with Marcie one more night, even though the snow had stopped falling for a bit, making it possible for him to come home. She shouldn't be alone on Christmas.

Suddenly, there was so much to do. I quickened my steps and wondered what Mama would say when I came to the door and she saw the cap on my head. And what would I say to her to make it all okay? Maybe I would tell her what I learned from Sadie, and the miracle of her chicks, and Ed, and Marcie, and even Mr. Darcey (who Mama would have to remember how to love, just like Marcie had to remember how to grow back her hair). It was what was left to do, and it was up to me to do it. I would tell her everything I knew: that everyone needs a someone, no matter who, no matter what the history. That is what I learned and that is what I would tell her. *Everyone needs a someone.*

Just then the wind whistled through the trees and a breath of new snow tumbled over the ice and then took into the air, as if sucked back up into the clouds from where it came. Everything went still. The trees no longer made music. The electric lines, usually swagged loosely between the pole lines, went stiff and brittle. I stopped running and inhaled deeply, or at least made the effort, but found the air knocked right out of me like a hard fall. It was then that I heard the first snap, as if someone had taken one step too far onto a half-frozen lake. Then it occurred to me: the sky. Gray. Black clouds. And Sadie. Just before she died. It was happening again. The very breath of God himself!

Shielding my eyes, I dropped down onto my knees and heard another snap from above, this one much louder, and felt the wind break against my back like a freshly cut switch. I knew what great event was happening above me. The sky had frozen solid and had cracked with enough force to stop the hearts of chickens and men.

But not mine.

• • •

That night, Plenty Porter tucked herself into a ball, forced her eyes closed tight, and whispered a single, powerful prayer—two words repeated twice—and in doing so, did not see that which Sadie saw.

"Not yet. Not yet."

PART THREE

In which Plenty Porter learns about maps,
and Marcie finally returns home

15.

THE TIME I gave Annie and Sam bloody noses at the same time—with only one punch, mind you—was the time that Sister Helen Rose took us all for a walk and put everything in perspective.

We were yelling at each other when Annie came at me and I curled up my fingers and made my knuckles protrude like spikes, and drove my fist into her nose, like a well-oiled piston. Her head snapped back, which was when the back of her head smashed Sam's beak, and both of them dropped to the ground, holding their bloody noses.

It was morning recess and we were still getting used to the fact that the snow had melted across the yard, giving us more room to play. The girls took the extra space to their advantage and tried jumping rope at the far corner of the yard, far away from me and Ed.

"What are they doing?" I asked Ed.

"Leave it alone, Plenty, they don't want to be our friends."

"That's silly," I told him. "We're wonderful people."

"We are?" Ed asked, and blushed. Ever since I invited Ed to Christmas dinner—the night I came home wearing Father's cap, the one that Mr. Darcey helped me pull over my head—Ed had been spending a lot of time with me: days, nights, sleepovers. He did this mostly because I invited him, which I reminded myself was a good deed to do. Ed needed a friend, and being that I was available most of the time, I'd let myself be that person. But mostly, I liked having him around, which was something I told Marcie once when I visited her in the hospital. I wrote on a piece of paper that day:

Here are some new things in my life. Ed is my friend now.

Marcie laughed at me. When I asked why she was laughing, she laughed again. If it weren't for the fact that it was good to see her laughing, I would have smacked her arm. Instead I kept reading.

Ed doesn't have a mother, which is why, I think, he's so strange. But I figure that sometimes strange can be good, so I let him come round as much as he wants.

And Marcie laughed again.

The thing that bothered me was that Ed was content with it just being the two of us, but I wanted more friends. My sister Rachel always had friends, lots of them, and I wanted most in the world to be like Rachel. This was why I went across the yard, freshly melted snow soaking into the grass, and tried to talk to Annie and the other girls at school. Ed walked at my side and I told him that he didn't have to come with me if he didn't want to, but he said, "They might as well hate the both of us now, they'll end up hating the both of us later. That's the problem with being your friend, Plenty. Somehow I always end up getting both the good and the bad."

The girls were playing jump rope again. Annie was sing-songing the same old words:

Lucy left the light on late at night
Polly put the pickle jar lid on tight
Home before supper
Not past then—

I skipped forward, jumping into the rope and finished their chant, "Or you'll take a trip with the Gentleman!"

The girls dropped the rope and it fell to my feet, coiled like a snake napping in the grass. "What are you doing?" Annie asked me.

I ignored the question. "Want to know something?"

"No," Sam said.

"Ed and me know about a girl who took a trip with a Gentleman and nobody has ever heard from her since," I continued.

"That's great, Plenty, now why don't you and your boyfriend go find some Negroes to play with and leave us alone," Annie snapped.

Negroes? I thought. "Negroes?" I asked.

"We saw you two after school," Sam said. "We followed you over to that juke joint and saw you go inside to talk to that colored man. My daddy says to stay away from you, no matter what kinda bet we made."

Ed grabbed my arm and pulled me away, "C'mon, Plenty, let's go."

"No, wait!" I said, coming at them. "You got something to say against Charlie?"

"Who the hell's Charlie?" Annie asked.

"It's her colored friend," Sam said. "Let's go."

Then the girls started to walk away from me. They walked away from me not because of Ed, not because I was from Alexis and was too tall, but because of my secret friend. I yelled at them, "Wait!"

And then I heard Annie say it, and Sam laughed and repeated what she said: "She's as crazy as her sister."

Without thinking, which is usually how things like this happen, I reached down and snatched up the jump rope in a big clump and threw it over their heads. It flew through the air and slammed into a window of St. Joseph's, the two handles hitting the glass in such a way that it cracked, held for a split second, and then shattered into bits. Annie and Sam and the other girls turned to face me, shocked at my temper. But it was too late. I came at them with one punch, hitting Annie square in the nose, causing her head to snap back straight into Sam's face. Then I pounced.

Sister Helen Rose had to pull me off of them because, well, I was a Porter and we don't stop until we get tired, and I wasn't tired yet. She was asking what we were doing fighting each other. "She just up and hit us for no reason," Annie said.

"For no reason! You saying there was no reason is enough to give me another reason," I said, coming forward again.

Sister Helen Rose pushed me back and started helping Annie and Sam up from the ground, telling them to keep their noses elevated. "They said Marcie was crazy and my friend Charlie is colored," I said.

"He *is* colored!" Annie yelled.

"That's not what you meant by it!" I said back.

Sister Helen Rose grabbed me by the arm, too, and soon all of us were inside the classroom during recess. "You girls can't see anything but yourselves," she kept on saying. Then she started pulling maps out of her desk. We didn't say anything else. We watched as she found more maps stuck behind a shelf filled with books on frogs and other animals. When the others came back into the classroom she held up her hand and said, "Stay outside. We're not done being outside yet."

Sister Helen Rose set a map of Galesburg down on top of a rock. The whole class was standing in the park that does not have a swing set, the one that just has trees and really looks nothing like a park, but more like a part of town where no one has built anything yet. She took a red marker and made a dot right on top of our school, or the place where our school sits, just off the town square. "That's our school." Then she made another dot, about a half inch away from the first dot. "This is the park. This is where we are." Then she drew a line between the two dots. "This is how far we've walked." Then she folded up the map and moved farther into the trees, without saying a word. Not long after, Ed started to follow her and then, one by one, we all left the rock and followed.

When we came to the river, which was the same river that went all the way into Alexis and beyond, Sister Helen Rose set the map down again and made another dot. We were now a good two inches away from the first dot. She said that she had planned on us all taking off our shoes and crossing the river, but being that it was spring and the snow had recently all melted, the water was too high. So, we continued walking down along the river until we came to a bridge. She showed us the bridge on the map, but it didn't look like a bridge. It looked like a squiggly line that was meant to be a road, cutting through a blue squiggly line that was meant to be a river. I guess we were learning about maps.

By the time we crossed the bridge, passed down the hill, avoided the train tracks, and made it to Route 150, each of us was exhausted. "Are we going to have to walk all the way back?" Sam asked, still pinching the top of her nose. Sister Helen Rose did not answer. She bent down and unfolded the map on the pavement. We all huddled around. She made a dot along a much thicker line, which was Route 150. It was a relatively straight line, meaning that it didn't make sharp turns like the others we had traveled along. Sister Helen Rose made another dot and then connected the last of the lines. We'd traveled six inches. I was amazed. Just by walking, we had nearly covered one half of the map.

Then Sister Helen Rose took another map from her bag and unfolded it on top of the first one. "This is our county," she said. She pointed out a shaded area that was Galesburg and made a dot at our school. Then she made another dot at Route 150, which, I learned, traveled all the way through the county. Then she connected the two dots. The space between the two dots only covered about one inch. Suddenly, it didn't seem like we traveled very far at all.

Then Sister Helen Rose unfolded another map. It was the state of Illinois. She was able to find Galesburg, which already had its own dot printed on the map. I asked, "Where's Route one-fifty?"

"Route one-fifty isn't a big enough road to be on this map," she said.

The last map she showed us was of the United States of America. It was big and rectangular. I had seen this map many times before. But this time I noticed something that I'd never noticed before: On the map of the United States of America, Illinois was only the size of a grown man's thumb. And when I got real close to it, I could see that Galesburg was not printed on the map. There wasn't even a dot. The river that roared between Alexis and Galesburg was only one of hundreds of hair-thin blue lines that cut like veins through the entire state, the entire country. Everything that I had ever known was so small.

Sister Helen Rose folded up the rest of the maps

without saying another word. She folded them up and put them in her bag and walked back toward the river. A truck drove by on Route 150 with a big load of cargo covered with a ripped brown tarp. I wondered how far that truck would go. By the time I looked away from Route 150, Sister Helen Rose and the class were already fifty yards away from me. Ed stood at my side. He was waiting for me, but he said no words. I thought about the notion of fifty yards. On the map that is our country, fifty yards is nothing. I thought about the place on the pavement where I was standing and guessed that the area I took up was less than twelve inches in every direction. On the map that is our county, on the map that is our town, twelve inches in any direction is nothing. No matter where I went, no matter what I was doing—lying, sitting, jumping, fighting—the space I took up could not even be measured.

When I looked up again, away from Route 150, the rest of the class was now one hundred yards away from me. I noticed that the farther they walked away, two girls were not moving with them. They were standing stationary. I knew it was Annie and Sam who were standing there, because they were still playing with their noses. And the farther the class walked away from them, the more it became clear that Annie and Sam were waiting for us. It was the day that Sister Helen Rose took us on a walk that we put everything in perspective. And afterward, Annie and Sam were waiting for me and Ed to catch up with them.

16.

FATHER HAD started working nights at the beginning of the new year. It was 1953 and I was still having trouble remembering to put the "3" on the date at the top of my schoolwork. Sister Helen Rose circled the "1952" that I kept writing on my assignments, and I swore to myself that I'd remember on the next one, but usually didn't.

He started working nights because Marcie had begun to grow some of her hair back. Mama said, "She's getting better. We have to keep her there so she'll *keep* getting better."

At supper one night, she mentioned that maybe Father could ask Mr. Prindergast to loan us some money. Father slammed his fork on the table and went outside. He didn't say why he slammed his fork. Sometimes it's like I miss the thing that makes Mama or Father mad at each other. Everything is normal. And then everything is not normal.

After supper, Mama found Father sitting outside

on the back porch smoking his pipe. She kissed his forehead and he put his arm around her waist. He said, "Never in front of the kids," and then she sat on his knee and the two of them looked out at the field. That was the nature of fighting between Mama and Father. One of them would shout or cuss or stomp real loud. Then they'd walk away. By the time they met up again, everything was healed and they'd cuddle some.

I'd been trying to think of a way to bring Mr. Darcey back to the house ever since Christmas. But nothing seemed right. I'd hoped that Mama would have seen the cap on my head when I came home from Mr. Darcey's house Christmas night. But she said nothing. She let me wear the cap all night long, but didn't say a thing about it.

It wasn't until the snow melted and Sister Helen Rose took us for a walk to put things in perspective that I had the idea. I told Ed all about my idea. I told him that once there was a stray dog that kept coming to our house looking for food. Mama started leaving scraps outside. The dog usually came and ate them at night when we were sleeping, but every once in a while, we'd see him wandering around the cornfield. I wanted to pet the dog real bad, but every time I tried to get near him, he'd run away. Jerry taught me a trick, because Jerry did things like that from time to time. He'd teach me something that I didn't yet know, and then walk back to one of the cars he was working on, like what he'd done was no big deal. He went inside the house and grabbed a couple slices of ham. Then he ripped up the ham into bits and made a trail of meat from the porch out into the yard. He put a big slice of ham inside my hand and told me to hold it out when the dog came round. Sure enough, the stray dog showed up a little bit later and started eating the ham, following the trail all the way to the porch, where I was sitting. I held out my hand, hoping he'd smell the meat inside, and kept real still. The dog tried to resist the smell, but couldn't. He kept getting his snout real close to my hand, to where I could almost feel his breath, and then he'd back away real fast. But I kept my hand out, held it real, real steady, and pretty soon he ate the meat from my hand and let me pet the back of his head.

Remembering that lesson gave me the idea to use something to draw Mr. Darcey out of his house, which is why I told Ed. "I don't understand," Ed said.

"I didn't expect you to," I told him.

"But you have a plan?" he asked.

"Yes, Ed, I have a plan."

At first I thought about stealing liquor out from Father's cabinet and making a trail of bottles from our house to Mr. Darcey's. But somehow that didn't seem to be a good idea—and besides, Father didn't have enough bottles and I didn't have any money to buy more. Whatever it was that I used needed to work in two ways. One, it had to get him out of the house and interest him enough to keep on walking. Two, it needed to somehow put things into perspective for him, just like Sister Helen Rose's map did for me and the four girls who used to call me a freak because I was too tall and were now my friends.

Mama kept an album full of old photographs in the table next to her bed. She used to say, "There's life in this album." So, I grabbed Ed and we snuck into her room one day when she was visiting Marcie and went through the album. There were pictures of all of us kids on the inside. We were pasted onto the stiff paper in no particular order. There seemed to be more pictures of the younger kids than there were of Bob and Dean and Rachel, probably because cameras became less expensive as the years went on. At the back of the album, I found a yellowed envelope that I'd never noticed before. I opened the envelope and removed a small stack of *really* old pictures, most of them faded terribly because they were so much older than the ones of us Porters. They were mostly of a little girl I did not recognize, even though she looked a lot like me when I was little.

"Who is she?" Ed asked, trying to grab them from my hand.

It wasn't until I reached a picture of the tenant house and the man who was the little girl's father that the stack of pictures made sense.

The next night, I got out of bed and snuck outside, which was something I was getting really used to doing.

That afternoon, Ed and I had stacked a few sticks of

wood under the porch where nobody would find them. I grabbed one, using it as a walking stick. Being that it was almost summer, the nights were getting sticky. Ed was waiting for me next to the tree that grew up beside his bedroom window. "You ready?" he asked me. I nodded and started walking. By the time we made it to Mr. Darcey's house, my clothes were damp. The lamps were not burning inside his house, which meant that Mr. Darcey was sleeping, just like I wanted him to be. "This is where he lives?" Ed asked, looking scared. "My dad says I shouldn't come to this part of town."

"You can turn back if you want, Ed."

"I didn't say that, Plenty. I was just asking."

"Okay, then keep low and follow me," I said, and crept into the clearing between his house and the river. I stabbed my walking stick into the ground until it was deep enough to stand up all by itself. "Give me the picture," I told Ed. He dug a picture out of his back pocket and gave it to me so I could tack it to the stick, which was now a post.

Walking back to our house, I wished I could be there when Mr. Darcey first saw the post and went outside to investigate. I wondered what he'd think when he saw a younger version of himself wearing an Army uniform, just before he went to fight in the trenches.

The next few nights, I rose at the same time, grabbed sticks from under the porch, and went off with Ed at my side. Each night we didn't have to travel as far, because we were making a trail with pictures, just like Jerry taught me to do with ham. It took nearly two weeks for us to finally bury a stick in the dirt at the top of Shanghai Hill, which would be the last picture I'd post, because it had a view of our house.

The next day was a Saturday, something I had planned because I wanted to be home when Mr. Darcey made it to the top of the hill. Ed and I laid out all day and read books to each other, all the while keeping an eye on the top of the hill.

But Mr. Darcey never came.

"Maybe he doesn't want to be helped, Plenty," Sister Helen Rose told Ed and me the next morning when I showed up at the convent crying.

My family had gone into Galesburg to hold church with Marcie, which the hospital did every Sunday morning, and Ed came along.

When we got to St. Joseph's, I told Mama that Ed and me wanted to go and find Sister Helen Rose, and she told us that was fine.

The nuns lived behind the church and the school, in a stone building that looked like an old castle. Ed knocked on the door, and a nun who I did not recognize answered. She didn't seem happy to see us. She said we could wait outside and she'd try to find Sister Helen Rose. We sat on a bench in the courtyard and watched a hummingbird hover around a yellow flower, plucking pollen with its beak. I wondered how hummingbirds knew where to find flowers and thought that maybe God left a trail of pollen dust that normal people can't see, floating in the air for hummingbirds to follow.

"What are you two doing here?" Sister Helen Rose asked as she came outside and sat on the bench between us.

"I finished another book," I told her, which was a lie.

"Is that what you came to tell me?" Sister Helen Rose was not wearing her habit this morning. I'd never seen her hair before and was surprised at how long and red it was.

"No," I said. "Not really."

Mass was starting inside church. I could hear the organ, but could *feel* it even more, rumbling the ground. The music made me sad, which I told Sister Helen Rose was the reason I was crying. She rubbed my back like Mama had never done, because it had never been done to Mama, which got me thinking about Mr. Darcey, who had never rubbed her back, and probably never would since he didn't follow the trail of memories that I had left for him. That was when I told Sister Helen Rose about Mr. Darcey. And right after I finished talking, she told me, "Maybe he doesn't want to be helped, Plenty. You can't force people to want to change. You can only leave the door open and hope they do."

This wasn't what I wanted to hear Sister Helen Rose say. I wanted her to give me advice, to tell me the thing that I should have done to get Mr. Darcey out of his house, the thing that would have worked. Instead, she told me to leave a door open, which didn't make sense anyway because the whole time I left it open, animals and bugs could get in the house, which Mama wouldn't have.

"But," Sister Helen Rose said, "there is something noble and selfless in what you both tried to do. You shouldn't stop because your grandfather didn't react the way you wanted him to. Keep thinking of other ways to help people. Think of some things your brothers and sisters might need, and try to help them."

"I don't know what they need, Sister," I said, which I knew to be true right after I said it. There were ten others in the house—well, nine, really, since Marcie had been at the hospital. And truth be told, I know Ed better than I do any of them, which I told Sister Helen Rose.

"It's true," Ed said, "Plenty knows me the most." It occurred to me that Jerry, Joyce, Martha, Rachel, Bob, Dean, Debbie, Peggy, and Johnny all had lives just like mine, all going on at the same time. Maybe their lives were worse, maybe better, but I didn't know anything about them.

"Everybody has a story," Sister Helen Rose told us. "With all the books you both read, you ought to know that by now."

Lying in bed that night, I asked, "Hey, Joyce, do you got a story?" But she just rolled over and started snoring.

• • •

In the morning, Mama dropped a pot.

I went into the kitchen and saw that the back door was wide open and a pot of spilled water was on the floor. Once I was at her side, my bare feet sloshing in the water, I saw that she was looking down to a clump of wildflowers held together by a string, resting on the porch. Attached to the string there was a picture of a little baby sitting on the floor of a room in a white dress. I knew the baby to be Mama, but I'd never seen the picture before. Mama stepped over the flowers and went out into the yard, spinning in a circle, looking for someone who might be watching.

I did not follow. I ran through the house instead, all the way to the front door. I threw open the door and ran to the mailbox, yelling, "Ed, come out here!" as I ran. He came quickly, right out the front door without his shoes, and joined me at the mailbox where we could see up to Shanghai Hill. Mr. Darcey was standing at the top of the hill with one of my posts in his hand like a walking stick.

"Is that him?" Ed asked. I waited for Mr. Darcey to see us, and when he did, I waved. He stood there a while longer and then turned around, walking slowly back down the hill.

"That's him," I said.

17.

MARCIE CAME HOME from the hospital just in time for the dance. Her friends had not seen her, but her hair had grown back and there was nothing that could keep her from going, even though it was likely she had been forgotten.

The doctors said it would be all right for her to spend some time out of the hospital, and father pledged to drive her into town every other week for what Sally liked to call "their sleepovers." Marcie needed an occasional sleepover, just to talk, to rest, and to remember again what it was she was striving to accomplish: A normal life, which seemed to mean a life in which she had all her hair, at least most of the time.

The local churches, including that of my school, St. Joseph's, gathered together at the end of each summer to plan a back-to-school dance that would make everyone happy—the kids, the parents, the priests, and the pastors. Mama decided, after we called her out on all the "walks" she had been taking over the summer—the ones that everyone knew ended at Mr. Darcey's tenant house—to join the dance committee and get back into the business of family.

But after two committee meetings, Mama decided it wasn't worth listening to the committee go on and on about how many inches between hips there'd have to be (and the detailed plan of enforcement) during the dance. Instead, Mama spent her time at home, making Marcie a dress for the dance, one that was green with white stitching. Mama and I picked out the pattern on a shopping trip to Monmouth. She thought we should get string that matched the fabric, which would be green, but no spool seemed an exact match, so I said, "Let's use white," which Mama resisted until I showed her a magazine with a picture of a girl in a similar dress who did not look like Marcie, but was her age and looked happy, and Mama then said, "Yes."

It was two days until my birthday and all I could think about was how Marcie would look that morning when she rose from her first night's sleep back in our house and saw the dress hanging in the closet. It was my job that night to remember to get the dress inside the closet once Marcie was asleep, and I took the responsibility seriously. Ed and me practiced the day before, twice, him lying in the bed pretending to snore while I carefully slipped out of the bed, trying not to rustle the covers or shimmy the mattress. "I'd sleep right through it," Ed told me, but I made him go through the whole thing one last time, just to make sure.

That night, I thought Marcie would never go to sleep. She kept rustling under the covers, shifting and spinning, until finally Rachel got up from the bed and sat at the window, smoking in such a way that made Marcie feel bad and go downstairs to lie on the couch. "Why'd you go and do that?" I snapped at Rachel and jumped out of bed, reaching under the boxspring where the dress was laid out flat along the floorboards, waiting to be hung. Truthfully, I didn't care much that Rachel had made Marcie feel bad about her tossing all night long—not much longer and I would've probably done the same thing. But I had been excited to pull off the operation that I'd practiced that morning, and now that Marcie was downstairs, I'd never get the chance to complete it as rehearsed.

Rachel flicked her cigarette butt out the window and went back to bed while I hung the green dress in the closet without ceremony. I thought about getting back to bed myself, but something caught my eye out the window, something moving near the trees.

It wasn't Marcie I saw out there, which came as some sort of relief. It had only been a year since I'd seen my crazy sister trembling out in the trees. There was no way of telling who it was, but someone was there nonetheless, pestering the ground between the grove and the cornfield with constant pacing. Certain shapes in the dark are hard to figure out. A shrub can be a coyote, a coyote can be nothing more than a house cat. From a distance in the dark, anything can be everything. I went through the list of possibilities of what this dark figure could be. And then, in the course of a yawn, my own, that same figure was gone. Everything went dark and my eyes filled up with stars, and when they cleared there was nothing left but the trees and the fields and a house that, even with me inside, was very, very quiet.

"What's the point in going to a school if you don't go to none of the functions?" I asked Ed.

"I'm not saying I won't be going. I'm just saying I can't help you do the decorating. I got to go into Springfield," he said, crossing from the mailbox toward Mr. Prindergast's car, which idled near the road.

"You don't *got* to do nothing. Your daddy wants you to go to Springfield, but if you wanted to bad enough you could tell him you had other stuff to do."

"But I don't have other stuff to do," Ed said. "You have other stuff to do and you don't want to be alone to do it."

"Not true," I said, "not true at all," and I walked away from Ed without saying good-bye. There was too much to do that day to stand around trying to get him to take part in society. Marcie was going to have her unveiling at the dance and I'd promised Sister Helen Rose that I'd hang streamers in the entryway to the gymnasium. I had fought for purple streamers since, in my mind, purple went better with green than red. I wouldn't want Marcie to stroll through a web of red streamers wearing a green dress and have her first impression—back at school and in the company of her friends—to be that of a walking Christmas ornament.

I'd told Ed he could come along and help me decorate, thinking that it'd be good for the boy to be around kids our age outside of the classroom. "Maybe everyone'd stop thinking you're such a brownnoser if they saw you doing something other than handholding every damn nun who happens to ask you a question," I told him.

"I don't hold anyone's hand anymore."

"Not literally," I said.

"Then what?"

"Huh?"

"That's my whole point, Plenty, you don't even know what you're talking about half the time you're talking."

"Then it's a good thing I have you around to clear things up, isn't it?" Ed took a pause. I smiled. "That's *sarcasm*," I said, "want me to define it?"

Truth of the matter: I was just mad 'cause he insisted on having other, more important things to take care of, things that did not seem to involve me.

Mr. Prindergast's car rolled slowly across the yard, tires crunching gravel like a thousand snail shells. Father had just gotten home an hour before and was likely fast asleep, so there was no asking him for a ride into Galesburg. Bob and Dean were busy in the fields. Mama was upstairs pinning the green dress to Marcie's bony hips for last-minute alterations. The only person left to ask was Jerry, and being that he'd just fixed up an old Ford, I was pretty sure he'd love the chance for a drive.

"I'd love the chance for a drive," Jerry said, and reached across the seat to open the passenger door. "Handle doesn't work from the outside."

We were speeding along Route 150 and the windows were down, Jerry was talking over the roar about his new Ford having "a supercharged flathead eight that gives it a hundred and fifty horsepower, which is enough to get ya airborne if this baby had wings," not to mention that it was not just purple, it was "eggplant purple, with a charcoal gray interior—" All that just to say that it was fast and loud and Jerry was feeling pretty good about himself.

And so was I.

Sister Helen Rose was outside the Corpus Christi High School gymnasium talking to Pastor Simon, and I thought it funny that they were both followers of God, but Sister Helen Rose never got to do it with a man, while Pastor Simon was married and had five children, which meant he'd done it at least five times. I wondered if Sister Helen Rose ever got jealous that Jesus let some people have relations, while other people, I guess, he didn't. Not that sex was much of an issue for me yet, but I have sisters and they get to talking, and it doesn't take a genius to realize that there is a point to holding dances—a secret point that nobody likes to admit; and that is that young people want to get to know other young people, and someday those same young people will be a little bit older and will grab on to each other and not let go, and that the act of grabbing and holding will end up bringing more young people into the world. All of it is a cycle, and it all somehow leads right back here, to a nun and a pastor standing around talking about where to place the punch bowl inside some gymnasium that smells like burnt onions so that it won't get in the way of the dancing.

Hours passed, afternoon came and went, and Sister Helen Rose brought in sandwiches for all us girls who helped with the decorating. I was eating with an eye on the door. "What are you looking at, Plenty?" Sam asked.

"Waiting for my sister to get here, that's all," I said, which was true, although not *completely* true. I was also waiting for Ed. Don't know why. Guess it seemed like he should be there, being that it was turning out to be such an important day. It was as if my birthday was coming early and would spread itself clear on through to the actual day. Tonight Marcie would show herself, and all the whispering—the gossip, the jib-jab that people did around town, in the schools, juke joints, and beauty parlors—would all come to a grinding halt and the Porters would finally be the center of attention for something other than the word "crazy." Once again we could go back to just being "too damn tall." And something as good as that might as well be celebrated like my birthday, since good things were bound to happen along with the number thirteen.

I left the gymnasium and took a walk alone through the dark halls of Corpus Christi High. Five girls, all older than me, stood together around the corner smoking; I could smell smoke before I saw the smokers. They were talking about Marcie.

"Will she be wearing a wig?"

"I heard her hair grew back."

And standing there in the hallway, listening to the smoking girls talk, I became angry because I knew that deep down they wanted it to be a monster movie—wanted Marcie to show up with no hair so they could point like she was one of those animals with two heads that travel with the carnival.

Back in the gymnasium, someone started playing records and the five girls took off down the hall, gliding right by me without even noticing that I was a Porter—just like Marcie. Outside, everyone was arriving in packs. I thought about their arrival like that, like packs of animals arriving to the water hole in a jungle somewhere, in a country much different from ours. I heard them through the walls, cackling like wild birds, cars and trucks roaring like lions in the parking lot. Suddenly these thoughts made my stomach turn, as if I'd walked right into something entirely different without knowing.

But then I became happy. Because Marcie would likely be here by now, and she would be beautiful in the green dress with white stitching. She would prove them all wrong with her pretty dress and confidence. We would all be there with her, all of us Porters, ten brothers and sisters and two parents. We'd all be there at her side. I became so happy right then that I started to cry. It was the kind of crying that comes when you're smiling so big and laughing so hard that it feels so good it hurts.

I walked back down the hall to the gymnasium, stopping only to pick up a book of matches that had fallen on the floor next to a long row of lockers. The book was red and none of the matches had been used. Gold letters spelled the word JUG'S in cursive script on the front cover. And were it not for the matches, the ones that had fallen on the floor, that I picked up, I probably wouldn't have noticed that the door to Marcie's locker, the one that had been given to her one summer past because we'd been there swimming so often— number 512—had been left wide open.

18.

FATHER CAME to the dance on his way to work his other job. He parked near the back of the lot to make sure that no one blocked him in from behind. His hair was still wet when I saw him coming from his truck. I had been looking for Marcie when Ed drove up with his dad. He asked if we'd be able to give him a ride home since his pa didn't feel like sticking around.

I said, "Hold on, I'll ask," and ran into the parking lot, which is when I saw my father coming from the Dodge, his hair wet and neatly combed.

"Can we give Ed a ride home after the dance?" I asked without even saying hello.

"It won't be me. I got to get to work, but I'm sure your mother will be happy to give you both a ride," he said, and I skipped on back to Mr. Prindergast's car to tell Ed the good news.

Ed got out of the car carrying a big net for catching butterflies that his pa bought him in town that day. I grabbed the net out of his hand and started running, hoisting it up high in the air. Ed ran after me, yelling, "Wait! There's no butterflies out this late!" But I didn't feel like thinking about that, the absence of butterflies, and kept on running.

The parking lot was pretty much full by then, with cars of all sorts. Running around, weaving in and out of the parked cars, with Ed stalking after me like a wounded animal—gasping and coughing and wheezing the farther we ran—everything was right once again.

This was the evening as I had seen it on all those sleepless nights, lying on top of the covers, thinking about Marcie's homecoming and my thirteenth birthday. "I wish I never had to go to sleep!" I yelled back to Ed as I ran, laughing as I swooped the net down and around and over my head.

"Are you drunk?" Ed hollered back.

I saw Mama meet Father at the door to the gymnasium and changed directions. I crisscrossed my right leg over the left, tucked my chin, and cut across the parking lot right toward them. Mama linked arms with mine and the two of us spun in a circle, right there, in front of the gymnasium, like she was a twelve-year-old girl who was just about to turn thirteen herself. Father laughed like he does when Bob or Dean tells a joke, and I knew, right about then, that we were all there, all of us, all happy, all for one reason.

"Where is she?" I asked.

"In the bathroom around back, making sure she

looks right," Mama told me. "I think she wants to wait till all her friends are here to make the big entrance."

"Did you . . . give her . . . the dress?" Ed asked, panting at my side.

"'Course we did," I said.

"Why're you out of breath, Ed?" Mama asked.

"I was—"

"He has a *condition*," I explained.

"Well, maybe you two should slow it down some," Father said.

"It's fine . . . Mr. Porter . . . I'm fine." Ed was still gasping.

"C'mon!" I said, and took off once again, flying into the tall grass at the side of the school where a bunch of fireflies dangled in the air like they were held by invisible string.

"Hold on," Ed said, grabbing my arm. "Look." Ed was pointing to the place next to the bathroom where those same five girls were standing underneath the small window. One of them hoisted another up onto her shoulders so she could see into the window, while the rest of them covered their mouths, choking back laughter. "What are they doing?" Ed asked.

It didn't need telling. I gripped the butterfly net with two hands until my knuckles turned to snow-capped mountains, and wielded it like a bat, running and whooping, swinging the net in front of me so fast that it sang like a windpipe. The girls saw me, but it was too late. I came on fast and knocked through them like they were bowling pins.

The light in the bathroom went dark just as the girls scattered back into the parking lot, cussing the whole way. I tasted blood inside my mouth from an elbow that caught my jaw.

I walked back to the bathroom and asked, "You okay, Marcie?" at the door. She didn't say anything, but I could hear that she was crying some. "Don't get worked up over those girls—they're ugly to begin with." Again Marcie didn't say anything. I reached for the bathroom door and gave it a good push. The door swung open but was met by Marcie's foot with such force that the whole thing came right back at me, nearly knocking me down.

"Don't come in here!" Marcie yelled.

Ed was standing away from me, fidgeting with his pockets, and I backed away from the bathroom, telling Marcie to take her time and we'd all be waiting for her when she was ready to come out and show everyone in the gymnasium how good she looks. That's when I heard the laughing. It came from the parking lot. From the same five girls, huddled together, watching the whole thing, hunched over with hands on their knees, like the front line of the Chicago Bears.

"Plenty . . ." Ed warned.

But I was already gone. I was chasing after them again. It was all a blur of sweat and tears. I was coming at them and there was no stopping. They split up into opposite directions. There were five of them, but I was used to ten. I'd gone after each of my brothers and sisters at one time or another out in the cornfields during the summer, and not once had I ever emerged without taking at least one of them down. I was swinging the butterfly net, Ed's butterfly net, and they were fleeing with legs that hit the ground in the downbeat of the music that swelled from inside the gymnasium.

It wasn't until I felt the butterfly net, Ed's butterfly net, hit the hood of a car, snapping at the handle, that I stopped running. The girls dissolved into the night, like water into sand. Ed was at my side, picking up the two halves of the gift from his father, trying ever so hard not to cry, while I was running my fingers over the scrape, wide like a canyon, carved into the hood of a souped-up old Ford, the one that got me there that afternoon.

"Jerry—" I began when he came around the back of the Ford where he'd been sitting on the trunk with Gary Moberg and their buddy Pogues, which was where they'd been sitting when they saw the whole thing happen. He didn't look at the scratch, and didn't need to, really. He'd heard the sound the net made when it snapped against the metal of his Ford, which was like thunder, or the sound the sky makes when God's breath makes it snap.

Jerry slapped my face, right then and there, in front of his friends and mine, and told me to go on inside. He slapped my face red and then said, almost gently, "Go on inside, Plenty." My chest heaved. "Go on inside and get ready for Marcie."

• • •

This was how it was when Marcie first came into the gymnasium, when she walked through the entry with the purple streamers. It was loud. There was dancing. Even Sister Helen Rose was dancing with a boy of five. The room was spinning. It was not me who was spinning, it was not the people who were dancing who were spinning. We were standing in place. We were still. It was the room that was spinning around us like a top. This I was certain about.

Mama saw it first. Then the rest of them, the ones who were dancing. Maybe I saw it last. I was busy counting the number of times my cheek throbbed in a minute. By the time I saw Mama take Marcie's arm and attempt to lead her away, saying, "Come on, honey, let's go outside," the room was out of control. A gift that was once so beautiful—as perfect as a dance and the return of Marcie in a beautiful green dress (that Mama and me had made) could be—turned on me like the Devil, just as Mr. Darcey had warned.

The room was spinning; the walls were spinning so fast that they melted and turned to mud, and the only ones in the room, the only ones stationary, were the Porters. I could see them among the masses, could connect the dots and draw a line from me to each of them, and another line from each of us to Marcie. She was at the far point. She was standing alone, her makeup running, her hair frizzed like it does on humid nights. And she was not wearing green.

The dress Marcie wore was blue and hung from her shoulders like a burlap sack. It was at least four sizes too big. The sleeves were not long enough for the arms of a Porter. And the string of a badly frayed hem dragged on the floor as Mama led her away. Each of us Porters followed.

Turning back at the entry to the gymnasium, the purple streamers crackling above me in a breeze, I faced those people inside, the ones who were there for dancing but had stopped dancing. Their faces were gawking, making their features seem twisted like freaks in a circus. This is how I saw them. But it was not them I was seeing. Somehow I knew this. The gymnasium at Corpus Christi High School had turned into a fun house, and what it was that I looked back into was not a room full of people, but a room full of mirrors. And the freaks I saw were not them. It was us I was seeing.

19.

THE NEXT MORNING, I woke and there was one more day until my birthday. It was a long day, but there was very little inside it. Father called work and said that he would be late because he needed to stop by the hospital and talk to Marcie's doctors. He drove away that afternoon, after sleeping only a little, and Marcie sat at the window, up in our bedroom, chewing her fingers, watching the Dodge pull away from the house with the familiar skid and crunch.

I spent the day in front of the mirror, watching the left side of my face grow bright red like a sunburn and then fade, more and more, down to a rose blossom, as if I'd simply been blushing. No one came to check on me. All attention was on Marcie. And yet no one came to check on her, either. No one did much of anything, really. We were sleeping in a dream of the day before yesterday, when everything was good, or was going to be—just before it wasn't.

Ed came to the kitchen door and asked to play, but

Mama told him that today wasn't such a good day. He kept making sure I'd be around tomorrow. "It's her birthday, you know?"

And Mama said, "Yes." She knows.

But I wondered if she really did. I wondered if she even heard what it was Ed had said. Maybe if he had said my name, said the word "Plenty," maybe then she would have remembered.

As night came, I took a piece of stationery out from the chest in the living room and went to the typewriter, the Remington, and fed the sheet through the roller. I was thinking of Sister Helen Rose and the exercises she had us do every morning. "Free writing" exercises—the ones meant to open our brains up like a book and help us put everything in order. I typed with one finger at a time and watched the letters come together like a puzzle. I was typing a list, one that included all the events of the year. Plenty Porter's twelfth year.

After pulling the page out from the Remington, I tried sleeping some. But when I thought about yesterday, things began to hurt and I began to cry until Marcie told me to quit.

"It was yesterday, Plenty. There's no use crying about yesterday," Marcie said. I went downstairs for a smoke, to air out some on the porch in the cool, and passed the room of my brothers, and then Mama's room, thinking all the while that I was minutes away from another year and that none of it mattered—that the weight of my birthday was more than anyone could handle, including me.

The book of matches I used to light the cigarette was the last piece of the puzzle that had not yet been put together. The matches were from a place called Jug's Liquor, which was off Route 150 on the way out of town. It was a place where Mr. Darcey went from time to time. I knew this because he told me the last time I visited him, and because he lit his cigarettes with the same book of matches. Having a smoke outside on the porch, in the cool of the porch, I noticed that something had been written on the inside cover of the matches in black ink, written by hand, which is to say that I recognized the handwriting, because it had been written by Marcie. The word Marcie had written was "midnight." Without meaning to, I had found a clue.

The light of Ed's flashlight wobbled in the room on the top floor of his house—a room that I knew was his because I'd been invited inside once, not by Ed, but by his father. Ed did not want his father to choose his friends, but somehow it happened anyway. Mr. Prindergast chose that I travel to school with Ed every morning, and, in doing so, we became friends. Which was why I thought it would be okay to climb up the tree outside his window and see what he was doing, which I really didn't care about. I was thinking about other things. I was thinking about being with Ed because anytime I was with Ed, Ed seemed to be with me.

When I came in through the window, I grabbed the book Ed was reading from his hand, read the first line, which was "Call me Ishmael," which I said out loud. "First person," I announced, and Ed laughed at me and said, "So what?"

"So, I don't like that person as much. I like talking about me like I'm someone else." I threw the book down on top of Ed's bed. It bounced as if it were on a trampoline. Ed seemed to watch it rise and fall, as if something had been done—as if a great offense had occurred.

Ed did not want me in his room, did not want me smoking in his room, did not want me looking at the framed picture of his dead mother next to his door.

I climbed from the tree, but fell, scraping my knee, and ran to the street, looking back only once to see if he was following. Which he wasn't. I'd almost made it to the mailbox when he came from the front door in only his underwear, calling, "Plenty, Plenty Porter! Are you crazy, running barefoot and alone this late?" I could tell he was having trouble breathing, which almost made me happy because it meant that he had run down the stairs. I wanted to tell him about the book of matches, about Jug's, and invite him along, but I was crying. Snot-dribbling sobs. How long until *my* hair started falling to the ground?

Ed ran into his house, yelling, "You're crazy, Plenty Porter!"

And Father came home from work six hours too early, and he was not wearing a uniform, which was how I knew what it was that had happened without it ever needing telling. I crouched outside the window, my parents' window, and listened, and heard—which is to say, mostly, that I heard Mama cry. There were so many words inside the crying. Mama said, "She has to go back to the hospital, Ray."

"Yes, she does. She will, she will go back tomorrow."

"Who's going to pay for it?"

"There's a way. We'll find a way because there's always a way."

"But nothing changes. The food. The work in the field. The girls are growing and need new winter clothes. Plenty's birthday is tomorrow and we can't give her anything—"

"I don't know. I don't know what to say."

And Mama cried some more. And Mama hates crying. So I left the place outside their room where I had been secretly listening. I left the yard where our house was caught under the shadow of theirs. I left behind the spot where I buried Sadie's feathers and the mailbox that was never straight no matter how much straightening came its way. I heard what it was they said inside that room and took it like it was a gift, not mine, but theirs. My gift to them. One less mouth to feed. Which is why I ran.

Which is why I am . . .

But first there was the list. The one I typed on the Remington. It went down the page. It didn't matter the spelling. It didn't matter the words. It didn't matter if the punctuation was misplaced or was used too much or too little. None of it mattered. It was a list. It was typed. And it flowed together, the words against the page, like spilt milk on the floor. It filled in the gaps, it moved along the floor in the way that memories move, which is to say that it moved and kept moving; that it was diverted by splinters, by imperfections. But it also flowed back on top of itself until the whole surface was covered; it became something more than just spilt milk; more than memories, more than just words on a page. The list looked like this. This is how it was.

"Year twelve"

Marcie woke me up in bed, Marcie brought me a hand full of hair, I put the hair in my pocket, we got a lotter in the post that no body let me ~~reed~~ read, father drove us into town, I saw Charlie, he told me about Bob and DEan, Bob and Dean

got to come home before ever going to Korea which was where Mrs. Reynolds brother went, and I found a

pocket watch out under the trees and hid it in my pocket, got my face slapped by Mrs. Reynolds because I was to tall, and went to her brothers funral and learned a lotabout

dying, but Johnny found the watch and gave it to mama and ihad to go n give it back to Mr. Prindergast, he saw

Ed and me -- or me and Ed talking and thouht we should go to school together, and I got to be friends with the girls who still think Im ugley and then Marcie lost all her hair and went to the hospitle and got visited by Mr. Darcey who is my grandpa and we became friends because Sadie my chicken died and got to see God breeth and the sky snap. And me and Ed -- or ed and me got to be friends because he didn't have no mama and then Marcie came home and mama made a green dress for her to ~~where~~ wear but she wore a blue one AND THEN JERRY SLAPPED MY FACE REDand thatday, that horrible day became yEstrday, my father losthis job, and just like thatI became one too many. And

my
birthday
is
tomorow
and I will be

thirteen

20.

WHICH IS WHY I am running.

Ed is inside his house. I see the window at the top of his house and I wonder if he is watching me, if he sees me crouched down outside next to my parents' room, where I am secretly waiting for words to escape like a breeze. My father is saying, "We'll find a way; we'll find a way for Marcie to get better." But Mama is crying and I know that neither of them, my father or my mother, knows what will happen next. Which is true of all of us, myself included; true of Marcie back in the hospital, of Ed inside his room watching or not watching, but me most of all, Plenty Porter, who is too tall, too many, a burden too big for anyone to bear.

There are roads, many, and I think of this as I run. I think of the roads outside my house as they looked on the map Sister Helen Rose showed us in school: Shanghai Bend, Pole Line Road, Losey Street, and Clark Street, Route 150—roads that loop like streams, feeding into wider roads that merge into streets that are paved, and highways and interstates, all of them connected to places that are bigger and better and easier, much easier than here. These places, far outside of Illinois, are waiting to be traveled to, waiting for arrivals, for people like me to find a mode of transport to get them there. So this is why I am running, and this is what I am running to. Transport. A car and a driver. A Gentleman to take me away.

The road to Jug's Liquor winds along the river and passes Mr. Darcey's house—the tenant house in which Mr. Darcey has lived alone for many years. The fact that he is probably a regular at Jug's Liquor plays inside my head like a record, spinning and sun-warped; a message too garbled to understand. There he is in my head, Mr. Darcey, sitting at a table in the corner of the bar, noticing a young girl of sixteen walk through the screen door. How long did it take for him to realize that the quiet girl, too young to be alone at a bar in the late hours of the night, was his granddaughter, Marcie? I imagine that Mr. Darcey kept her safe, looked out for her, just like he did at the hospital, just like he would still be doing now if she were still there. I wonder if Mr. Darcey will be at Jug's tonight, there to notice a girl of *thirteen* years walk those first few steps, barefoot, on splintered planks of wood.

The front of Jug's Liquor is a bit of a lie. A large door fitted with red and blue stained glass welcomes visitors atop a wide stairway that leads to a porch built out like the perch of a pirate ship. But there are no hinges on the door because the handle and the hinges were removed years earlier to keep drunken Irishmen from slamming it shut with so much force as to break the stained glass. The patrons now enter through the back door, squeezing down a hallway used by the owner, Duke, as a storage space for boxes of bottles and canned goods. Nobody parks in the front of the bar any longer, making the place appear from the street to be closed for business, which I imagine suits the regulars—people like Mr. Darcey who is my grandfather—just fine.

I am walking around to the back entrance of Jug's Liquor—a tight-lipped screen door that does not shut properly due to an ancient frame. Inside, music pumps from a juke, rattling half-empty bottles into a jingle like a fat man doing a jig with loose change in his pockets. Walking up the gravel lot I begin thinking of all the new places I've entered and all the new people I've met over the last year since Bob and Dean first came home. By walking through the threshold of new schools and homes and cars, by meeting strangers with so many names, I have become something of a stranger myself, like a character in a book.

Weaving between a parked car and a delivery truck, I notice a short man with a queerly thin mustache snuff out a cigarette on the bottom of his shoe, drop it, and head back inside. A moment later, my bare foot touches down on the same cigarette butt. I press down on the butt with my heel and reach for the door, cautiously, until my brain registers a slight burn and there is nothing left to do but lift my foot and go on inside. And in the space of time between smashing the cigarette butt and pulling open the screen door, the person I have been and the outsider I figure I've appeared to be to everyone else, has transformed into the character that I am: Plenty Porter, thirteen years old less than thirteen minutes ago, a stranger walking into one last strange place, looking for a car ride to the end of things.

Plenty Porter stepped through the door of Jug's Liquor and wondered how hard it would be to get a drink.

It doesn't take long for her to be noticed, which isn't much of a surprise since she is thirteen and enormously tall. But the first thing the man with the thin mustache points out is her feet.

"Where are your shoes?" the Mustache Man is asking as Plenty makes it from the hallway into the bar, hearing the screen door slap shut behind her. His face is freckled like salami and when he speaks, a bit of tongue squeezes between a wide gap in his front teeth. "Where are your shoes, lady?" he asks again.

"Left 'em behind," Plenty says, and scans the room for a Gentleman.

"Let me guess," the man starts to say, but is interrupted by a belch—his own.

Another man, the one behind the bar, asks, "What're you two going on about?" Duke, who is the man who owns Jug's but also works the bar each and every night, is the man behind the counter. He turns to face Plenty—a stained rag and a dirty glass in his hands. Plenty recognizes Duke from places in town that she can't recall and wonders how it is she could know so many people to whom she's never been formally introduced. Duke has never stopped by the house, never played cards with her father on Wednesday nights. And being that he is a proprietor of alcohol and sin, as her Mama always liked to say, Plenty knows there is a real good chance Duke won't recognize her face any more than he would any other thirteen-year-old girl in town.

"I said, 'Let me guess,'" the Mustache Man repeats while waving away the stench of his belch. "A lady walks into a man's bar without shoes," he says, "and it gets me thinking that there's a story brewing."

"There is," Plenty says under her breath, letting her voice get lost under the hump of the juke. "There's a story brewing."

"Then her first drink's on me," the Mustache Man tells Duke, and gestures for Plenty to take a stool.

Plenty continues farther into the room, and the thought that maybe she has been mistaken for a grown lady makes her strain to see through the smoky haze, like a bride looking through her veil for an easy escape on the day of her wedding. Plenty notices a glass of tea-stained ice melting atop a small, unmanned table in the corner of the room—just the place where Mr. Darcey might sit. She wonders if perhaps Mr. Darcey is here after all; and maybe he will be the one who ends up taking her on the road.

By the time she takes a stool at the bar, Duke has already set down a glass filled to the brim with ice and a clear drink and tells Plenty, "Go ahead and drink up and tell us a bit of your story."

Plenty wonders if the liquid inside the glass will feel anything like Tabasco going down her throat, which might be why men make pained faces after taking a drink. Plenty hadn't ever thought about drinking alcohol until tonight, and the last thing she wants to do is give away her age by gagging like you would after drinking spoilt milk, so she says, "Okay," and fists the glass like a woman who isn't afraid.

The Mustache Man moves two stools closer and props his head in his palm, waiting for Plenty to begin. She smiles, puts the glass to her mouth, and keeps tipping it back until the liquid breaks the seal of her lips and slides down the length of her tongue. And it isn't until a chunk of ice falls against her teeth that Plenty realizes she is only drinking water.

"So, *young* lady," Duke is saying, "you want to tell us what it is you're doing here this late at night?" Plenty begins worrying that it'd be mighty easy for Duke or the Mustache Man to pick up a phone and ask to be connected to the Porter place, ending Plenty's journey out of Illinois before it ever really began.

"I'm looking," Plenty begins to say.

"Looking for what?" Duke asks.

"For a ride."

"You got somewhere you trying to get?" It is the Mustache Man now, leaning across the length of the bar, close enough that he could tickle her chin. Plenty says, "Yes," and asks for more water.

Duke obliges her request, fills the glass from a pitcher, and asks her, "Where?"

Plenty says she doesn't know exactly, and begins drinking, slow and steady, wishing all the while that there was no end to the water and that her mouth would remain too full to answer any more of their questions.

"Well?" Duke asks.

The glass is empty. Plenty wipes her mouth. "You got a john back there?" she asks, "I gotta pee."

"Not for ladies, but you can use the men's once Walt has cleared out of there," Duke says, giving Plenty the go-ahead to get up from the stool and start on back through the storage hallway and into the room with an indoor toilet. She wonders if Walt is the first name of Mr. Darcey and begins to be afraid that maybe Mr. Darcey will not like the idea of a young girl like her being out so late at night. Maybe he won't take her on the road, which makes her walk faster.

Duke is hollering, "You better get ready to fess up while you're in there, girlie," but Plenty is hardly listening, because the back door is only a few steps away from the lavatory and all she can think about is making a run for it before Duke gets her to tell them a piece of her name.

Picking up speed, Plenty sidesteps a box of canned

pineapple, passing the door with the word MEN written in black paint. The toilet flushes from behind the wall, water sloshing through pipes just over her head, and a hunched man steps into the hallway from the lavatory. This man is surprised to see a girl running outside, a bit of her face passing through the electric glow of a light fixed above the door. He darts down the hall and catches the screen door with his foot, calling, "Plenty, Plenty Porter?" which is the exact moment I knew he was talking about me.

"Hiya, Mr. Prindergast," I say, turning back slowly toward Jug's.

Mr. Prindergast, Ed's father, is standing half inside Jug's, checking over his shoulder to see if anyone is with him in the hallway. A clump of his bangs is matted to his forehead, and I wonder if it's water from the washroom or a night's worth of sweat collecting in his hair. Standing face to face with someone I recognize makes me feel safe again, which is a disappointment. This man is the father of Ed, meaning that he knows who I am, that I am no longer a stranger. Once again I am only just me.

"What are you doing here, Plenty?" he asks.

And there is an answer to his question, a specific answer that involves escape, but the possibility of Mr. Prindergast telling my father exactly what it is that I tell him in response causes me to think of other answers, ones that will satisfy Mr. Prindergast while saving my hide from the lash of a switch when I am back at home in the company of my father, which I have vowed never again to be. I figure Mr. Prindergast would likely take pity on me if my excuse for being in a place like Jug's, alone after midnight, stirs up a bit of sympathy within his sagging frame. So I start by telling him, "It's my birthday."

"So, what—you thought you'd come and get yourself a drink?"

"No, sir," I say. "Only drank a glass of water—you can tell by my breath. I came because of Marcie."

This makes Mr. Prindergast inhale deeply and walk one more step toward me, bringing the whole of him out of Jug's. He catches the screen door with one hand and leads it softly to the frame without a sound. "Your sister Marcie?" he asks.

"She used to come here at night, to be with my grandpa, Mr. Darcey—before she went into the hospital," I say. "Mr. Darcey used to come drinking here nights, but he's never admitted to meeting up with Marcie. I guess he and Marcie must've had some kinda pact, and that man never broke it. I found a matchbook from Jug's inside Marcie's locker, so that's how I figured it all out. I dunno, Mr. Prindergast. I guess I just wanted to walk around a bit—in her shoes, you know? Like my daddy says, it's good to try to see the other side of things sometimes, even if you don't really want to. Wanted to see Marcie's side of things, I guess, and maybe find something that could help her grow her hair back."

And just as I finish talking, a sneeze tickles down

the inside of my nose and I try to hold it there—just in case Ed told his pa that his friend Plenty sneezes every time she lies. But Mr. Prindergast quits looking at me like he caught me doing something bad and rubs down the sacks underneath his eyes. By the time I'm inside his car, he's already asked if I'd told my folks about Mr. Darcey and Marcie's late-night rendezvous, but I don't know the meaning of the word and tell him, "No."

21.

WE ARE DRIVING when Mr. Prindergast starts telling me about his wife, Ada Marie. It was something of a surprise to hear her name spoken aloud after so many months spent watching Ed do everything in his power to avoid any topic that might lead to the mention of his mother. But Mr. Prindergast seemed okay with the fact that his wife was dead because he was talking about her as if she were right there with us in the car.

"She's beautiful, isn't she, my wife?" Mr. Prindergast asks.

"I dunno, Mr. Prindergast," I say, looking straight back into my own eyes reflected against the window. "I've only seen one picture of her," I tell him, thinking of the framed photograph that hangs in Ed's bedroom.

"But in that picture . . ." Mr. Prindergast begins to say, letting his voice trail off like a ripple in a calm lake.

It occurred to me that maybe me and Mr. Prindergast

could strike ourselves a deal. Maybe he could drop me off on the road next to the mailbox and I could sneak back inside our house before anyone ever notices I'm missing. Of course, what I'm really thinking about is a second chance at getting away—another way out of town since Jug's didn't lead to any sort of meeting with any real sort of Gentleman. Mr. Prindergast and I could come to some agreement—me sweeping leaves from his porch in exchange for a little secrecy between us fellow late-night wanderers. I'd make a promise that I'd have no intention of keeping and by the time he got around to collecting on it, I'd already be gone.

But by the time I have it all figured out, the future secrets between Mr. Prindergast and me, he passes by our road without stopping and asks me to talk a little more about Marcie. Watching our two houses, his house and my own, as they shrink into the trees the farther we drive away, I ask him why he wants to know more about Marcie. She's been in the hospital for half of a year and Mr. Prindergast has done nothing at all to be of any help to her cause—something I overheard Mama mentioning to Father one morning just after Mr. Darcey started leaving a trail of pictures and flowers, leading all the way back to his house. A man like Mr. Prindergast, with all his land, could see to it that no one in his employ would ever have to fear for their family's well-being. It seemed to Mama, as I heard her say to my father (which I repeated to Jerry before he slapped my face red just the other day), that Mr. Prindergast was making more of a show by not inquiring into Marcie's health than he would if he simply sent flowers to the hospital. At least then it would have looked like he cared some, even though we all knew the real truth of the matter. Men like Mr. Prindergast don't have to care. They live in places beyond caring, where their place in the world, let alone that in Heaven, is assured. Their price has been paid, not by Jesus, but by the Bank of Illinois, just outside of Monmouth.

"I hear Marcie is going to go back to the hospital," Mr. Prindergast says.

"That's true," I say, and consider telling Mr. Prindergast that Father had to take a night job to pay for everything, but lost that job on this very night. But then I remember that it's not really Marcie's health that's the problem. It's the number eleven that has Father scraping to get by. Which is when I become certain that the most important thing, for my family and me both, is to lessen the numbers—for Plenty Porter to go away.

"Where are we going, Mr. Prindergast?" I ask.

"Just taking a drive," he says. "You know, I first met Ada Marie when I was not much older than you. We went to the same school, from high school on through graduation. I guess you could say we were childhood sweethearts. Most beautiful girl in school, Ada was, and I got her."

"Yes, sir," I say.

"Does Ed talk about her much?"

"Not much at all," I say. "But I think he misses her some. He's never said so, but I can tell. Sometimes he sorta just stares off, like he's sleeping with his eyes open, and I pretty much figure he's thinking about her."

"It's tough for the boy, I'd imagine," Mr. Prindergast says. "He never really got to meet her. I don't know what he thinks about when he tries to remember his mother. He's seen a few pictures of her, only a few, but each one was so heavily *posed*, so much so that I don't think Ed really has an idea of how beautiful she was. Do you know what I mean, Plenty?"

I do know what he means and I tell him so. I say, "Yes, I do, Mr. Prindergast. It's just like it is in our school pictures—they only let us smile so much." And after saying so, something in Mr. Prindergast's tone changes, as if we are becoming friends, which makes me feel a bit better. He is talking *to* me, listening and responding, like we are two friends who met at a bar, shared a laugh, and took a ride to keep the night from ending.

"That's right!" he says, slapping the steering wheel with the palms of his hands. "Just like those awful school pictures. Those aren't really you, are they, those photographs? Where's the dirty fingernails? Where's the slumped posture?" he says, which makes me wonder if he thinks *I* have slumped posture—something that Mama has been correcting since I started wearing britches. "It's just like Ada Marie," Mr. Prindergast continues. "I look at those pictures and I can't see the real her, and it makes me worry about Ed. When he tries to imagine his mother does she always have those horrible expressions? I want him to see how she looked when she laughed, so that he can make those pictures come alive in his head. That's what I try to do myself. I try to make them come alive."

And, I think, nothing could be more exciting than the thought of seeing a picture burst into life. How would it be to see Mrs. Prindergast's picture—the one in Ed's room—suddenly blink, or smile; see her chin drop and then lift like she was stretching after waking from a long dream; and then, as if from the act of moving, to witness a bit of color flow into those faded cheeks. How wonderful that would be! I am sitting in a car, driving away from my house, which is exactly what I wanted anyway, having a conversation about bringing the dead back to life. So much has changed just by becoming thirteen!

I turn in my seat, wrapping my feet Indian-style, and ask Mr. Prindergast if they do, if those pictures ever do come alive.

"Not like you'd think," he says, making a turn farther into the country. "They come alive one piece at a time. I'll hear someone on the street say something that reminds me of Ada's way of talking, or maybe I'll notice the way a woman lifts her skirt when stepping over a puddle, and suddenly she's right there with me again—just for a second."

"That sounds sad," I say to him. "Only getting to see her for a second's time."

And Mr. Prindergast tilts his head a bit to the side like he's not so sure, but resigns himself finally to the word "Yes."

"But . . ." And I knew there was a *but*, even before he said it. "But . . ." he begins to say, and slows the car, stopping along the side of the road on the uneven gravel next to a cornfield. "But sometimes—" He begins again, "sometimes you meet someone who so totally reminds you of the person you miss so terribly much, that there's no other choice but to bring 'em in close for as long as you possibly can, and say all the things you wish you would've said years before."

And in that moment I wonder if he is talking about me. We are stopped on the side of the road. Mr. Prindergast cuts the engine and the two of us sit quietly, listening to the cornstalks chatter in the breeze like they're cold. So much time goes by without us talking that I begin to think that maybe I'm being rude for not responding to him after hearing so personal and secret of a confession. I settle on something short, something simple, hoping to calm his worries, whatever they may be. "I understand," I say. I tell him that I understand. And, truth be told, I do.

Mr. Prindergast looks away from the steering wheel, perhaps for the first time, and his eyes are black holes without end that I am traveling up inside. Which is when it makes sense to me, the question I should ask, the only question that seems to matter any. "Are you a Gentleman, Mr. Prindergast?"

And with only one hand left on the wheel, the other waiting on the console between our two seats, he says back slowly, "Why yes, Plenty, I suppose I am."

22.

THERE IS SOMETHING he has to show her, something deep inside the cornfield, and were he not a Gentleman, Plenty might have thought it strange for a man his age to keep a secret buried inside a maze of cornstalks. There is no hurry in their walk from the car—nothing to indicate a race or a lack of time. The Gentleman was once a landlord to her family and now is something entirely different. His relationship to the girl is hard to define, as if there were multiple meanings stringing after a single word as printed and defined in a dictionary. She is aware of this, and she is aware that he keeps two steps behind her, watching that she not stray from the path set in front of her.

Far into the cornfield, Plenty makes the decision to stop walking and turns to face the Gentleman. She'd never been alone with a man who was not family and wonders if this is what's called a date. Debbie had been on many dates since high school, and once even said she and a boy went on a walk together. But that was Ronnie Taylor who played basketball and wore dirty sneakers, not a Gentleman who was tall, rich, and missing a dead wife. This evening was based on sadness, and somehow Plenty thought that no two people could be better suited. He might just understand her, understand those things that have set her apart from all the others without want, and, in the end, might just rescue her with his big, thick pocketbook and take her far away in his big, fancy car.

The Gentleman sees that she has stopped walking, sees that she is facing him now, caught with a cornstalk on each side, leaves blocking the black night sky. And seeing this, the way in which she has stopped, the way in which she looks at him, the Gentleman knows that she wants an answer, that there is no going farther without one. In the car he said that he had a secret, something he wanted to show her, out there in the field. She took the walk and yet also knew—deep down like a sliver of broken glass stuck in a foot, too small and clear to see, but *felt* nonetheless—that there was nothing out there, nothing waiting for her in that field except, maybe, an answer. Just by walking a few hundred steps into a cornfield, Plenty grew up a bit more and figured out that the secret, the thing he had to show her, all along, was he.

"What's this all about?" Plenty asks.

The Gentleman shakes his head and squats on the ground in front of her. When he finally looks up at her, she sees right into his face because they are now the same relative height, the Gentleman and the girl.

He keeps still, not talking, not answering her question, so she asks one more, "You're not taking me home, are you?"

"Do you *want* to go home?" he asks.

"Maybe not. Maybe I'm looking for a new one."

"Me, too," the Gentleman says, just as he starts to cry.

The Gentleman is crying, but not in a sad way—not in the way Plenty herself cried earlier in the night when she remembered yesterday. The way the Gentleman is crying is out of regret, or guilt, like he has done something bad, or is about to. Taking a step backward, away from the Gentleman, Plenty realizes that all along she knew that taking a drive with a fancy stranger—even if that fancy stranger was not a stranger to begin with, but became one later—was a mistake. All night she had been looking for a ride out of this place, looking to search through the country and find a spot big enough to hold her. But she hadn't considered that a man like that, one who drives cars and picks up little girls, even girls who are tall and thirteen, might want something in exchange for the trip. Watching this Gentleman cry, knees wobbling one inch from the ground, makes her remember the rules of the jump-rope chant that she should've adhered to:

"Home before supper," she says.

"What's that?" he asks. "I can't hear you." He places one big hand on the ground and uses it to lift himself back into a standing position. She backs away from him, picking up speed as she mumbles a nursery rhyme that he can hardly hear.

"Not past then—"

Stepping forward, reaching for her, he says, "Plenty . . ."

"Or you'll take a trip with the Gentleman."

She backs into a cornstalk, bending it down until she can't move any farther, and stops. He is close to her now, the grown man, the landlord, the father of her only real friend—the Gentleman. He has stopped crying and something in his face tells her that this fact, that he is no longer crying and is inches from her, is not good.

"Why are you doing this?" she asks, not quite sure what *this* is going to end up being.

"Because you know too much," he says, "and it's only a matter of time before you realize it."

Not long from now winter will once again rear its quiet fury. To Plenty, the thought of being around to see it becomes a mystery, immediate and essential. She knows that there will no longer be any escape this evening, not unless this was it, and the last place she'd see with living eyes would be a cornfield, not unlike the one in which she watched her father and brothers farm, year after year, from the room upstairs. Plenty is seeing things differently. With his crying and the sweaty gait of his walk, the Gentleman is a Gentleman no more. She can no longer picture him in Boulder, Savannah, New York, or Hollywood. He is no longer connected to places far away, as roads connect to highways. He becomes something smaller, simpler, and she sees him only as he is right then, a lonely landowner standing in a field. For this reason alone, she says his name, the entirety of it, and hopes that just as he is no longer a Gentleman, she'll no longer be a frightened little girl.

"Walter Prindergast," I say, and he steps back like he's been stung by a bee.

A car passes by on the road behind them. The light comes before the sound. It is as if the leaves themselves begin to glow bright white from their insides. Mr. Prindergast spins where he stands, trying to get a look at the car, and for a moment it is like we're caught in a black-and-white movie—everything either bright or dark, and nothing in between. The sound catches up with the car and passes on down the road, taking with it the white light. Nothing dims. It just moves away, hopping from one leaf to another, until it is gone.

Mr. Prindergast smoothes down the front of his shirt, tucking the tail back inside his pants. My eyes have trouble adjusting to the sudden lack of light, and when Mr. Prindergast starts coming toward me again, his face is an empty blot of nothing. His voice is saying, "Let's get this over with."

But I am talking at the same time, talking over him, telling him, "No, no, Mr. Prindergast, I'm too young for you to love me like you loved Mrs. Prindergast, I'm just too young."

And this makes him laugh. This makes him shake his head and laugh. "I'm sorry, honey," he says. "You have it all wrong. It's not you."

"Then who?" I ask.

He sighs and says, "It's Marcie. She's the one who makes the sadness go away."

And something in the saying of Marcie's name makes him seem light, like something had been lifted from his shoulders, which might have been how he got to me so quickly. The rest of it is like napping by accident. Everything around me is real: Voices, feelings, the stab of a twig into my palm when I fall—all of it is real and happening right then, and yet not happening because I am someplace else at the same time. There are arms around me and everything is dark and heavy and quick. By the time his fingers coil around my neck, my eyes are full of stars and everything is quiet. It's so quiet you could almost hear a single hair fall from Marcie's head—a single strand, blown from the palm of my hand like a broken wish, as it did the day this whole thing started, the day Marcie shared a part of her secret and offered me a handful of her hair. Before that, there must have been meetings, out by the trees near the field from where I'd see Marcie emerge, from where I once found Mr. Prindergast's pocket watch, which he must have dropped. It was he who visited Marcie up in that hospital room, not Mr. Darcey after all. He must've known the real Mr. Darcey would never show up, making him just the person to become. And that thing that Doc Wander said, that secret thing that kept Marcie from growing hair, appeared before me, jagged and bright as lightning.

And suddenly I am standing in Ed's bedroom, looking at the photograph of his mother, a photograph that is alive and full of color, noticing the brilliant blue of her old-lady dress—the dress she was wearing on the day the photograph was taken, a day when she was still alive. It was the dress that Marcie wore at the dance. Marcie must have worn that dress on other days, too—on the days she became someone else; the days she resurrected the dead.

Sadie is somehow chirping in my ear, and it is then that I see a figure, over the shoulder of Mr. Prindergast, standing in the distance. This figure walks through the field toward me, doing a little do-si-do around the cornstalks, with the open arms of an angel who has come to take me home.

There is a loud snap, just as I expected there to be, and I look to the sky and expect to see Heaven. But all I see are Mr. Prindergast's own eyes, inches from my own, wide and set apart on either side of his nose, painted over in gray pulp. His fingers slip from around my neck and my lungs suddenly expand as they're filled with hot air. Someone is saying, "Plenty, Plenty, are you okay?" but it is not Mr. Prindergast, or even Sadie, or any angel, for that matter. And just as I realize that Sadie no longer chirps in my ear, I realize that Mr. Prindergast is dead.

I pull my head from the ground and pin my chin against my chest, looking down the length of my thirteen-year-old frame just in time to see Mr. Darcey, not sitting on his porch, but standing here in the middle of a cornfield hovering over Mr. Prindergast, removing something from his back. It was that same thing, I suppose, that made the snap that was not the sky—that was not God—and killed Mr. Prindergast. Mr. Darcey leans down over me and winks without a word.

I say, "Hiya, Mr. Darcey," just as he scoops me up from the ground.

"I gotcha, Plenty," he says, and carries me straight out of the cornfield and to his own car, parked a few yards in front of Mr. Prindergast's.

"You have a car, Mr. Darcey?" I ask.

He says, "No, I borrowed it from a friend of ours." Mr. Darcey balances me on his knee and opens the door with one hand, setting me down on the inside, as soft and gentle as a good-night prayer.

And it is at that moment, while watching through the dirty windshield as her grandfather limps around to the other side of his car, that Plenty Porter is truly sure that she's finally met a real-life gentleman.

23.

THE NIGHT that Plenty Porter decided to run away from home, Ed Prindergast sat in his unlit bedroom, crouched down at the window, and watched Plenty head for the road.

He told Mr. Darcey later that night that she was barefoot, and that was the only reason Ed decided to follow after her. When Mr. Darcey asked Ed why he was crying, Ed told him that he'd gone all the way to Springfield the day before and bought Plenty a brand-new copy of some book about a whale, and had planned on giving it to her for her thirteenth birthday. But she snuck into his bedroom ten minutes before midnight, saw it on his bed, and tossed it aside like she'd plain forgotten how much she liked books. Ed didn't know what to get Plenty now for her birthday, and what was worse, she was running off into the night, alone and barefoot, and he didn't know if he'd ever see her again.

Plenty was much faster on foot than Ed, and being

that he was wearing only his underwear and a T-shirt, he clung to the dark edges of the road, embarrassed, just in case some car came passing. By the time he got to the fork at the end of the road, Plenty was out of sight and he was having a terrible time catching his breath.

Mr. Darcey found Ed on the way home from town, where he'd gone that day to trade stacks of wood in exchange for groceries and cigarettes. He'd borrowed a car from one of his neighbors, just as he did from time to time. He found Ed sitting on the side of the road, his chest held out tight and straight like a ply-wood sign fixed to his spine. Mr. Darcey stopped his car and called out through the window, "Don't be scared, youngin', I'm Plenty's grandpa. Remember me?" Ed nodded his head and got up from the road, dusting off the backs of his bare legs. Mr. Darcey asked him what he was doing sitting out in the middle of nowhere in only his skivvies, but Ed either didn't know what skivvies were, or he just didn't have enough breath in his lungs to get out any words.

"Needless to say, I got him inside the car and started to drive him home when he started saying your name, Plenty."

Mr. Darcey is talking while he drives farther into the woods, toward the river, toward the tenant house where he lives—the place the kids at school call Colored Town. Ed is laid out in the backseat taking real short breaths that sound like they hurt, his skin so blue he looks cold.

"You're lucky he was so hell-bent on going after you," Mr. Darcey says, "else I might never have seen that car parked on the side of the road."

Everyone needs an ally, I think to myself and maybe say aloud, although I'm not sure.

It occurrs to me then that the car belonged to Ed's pa, and Ed's pa was the one who Mr. Darcey used his knife on, so I ask if Ed saw the car that Mr. Darcey saw. But Mr. Darcey shakes his head and says that Ed's been pretty much asleep this whole time and if we don't get him a shot of adrenaline soon, he might not wake up. Yellow light flickers up ahead and I know that we're close to Mr. Darcey's home. I say, "It's good he didn't see it, Mr. Darcey. That was his pa back there."

Mr. Darcey whips his head around at me real fast and says, "*That* man . . ." but doesn't finish the thought. Mr. Darcey killed a rich man tonight, while protecting me. Up until the moment we pull in near the mill, into Colored Town, and Mr. Darcey starts honking his horn for help, it hadn't occurred to me what exactly that meant. Mr. Darcey's neighbors come running from their wood cabins wearing only their undervests and nylon caps. Mr. Darcey jumps out of the car and pulls Ed out from the backseat, hollering real loud that the boy's not breathing and has turned himself blue. I watch from inside the car as a half dozen or so men, and the women who were watching from the windows inside the lamp-lit cabins, move outside and swarm around Mr. Darcey, taking Ed from his tired hands.

They put Ed in the arms of another man, a man I

recognize quite plainly. It is Charlie, my friend Charlie, not standing outside the Apple-O, but standing outside his house, which is just a short walk from Mr. Darcey's.

"Hey there, Charlie. Brought back your car, but found this little guy along the way," Mr. Darcey says. All along they've been neighbors, my grandpa and my colored friend. All along I could have simply asked Charlie to tell me about my grandpa, but for some reason I never made the connection. Mr. Darcey had to live far away from town because he was poor and a drunk, and Charlie had to live there because he was colored. Guess it makes sense that they'd end up friends.

Mr. Darcey does not go inside. He takes a couple men his age by the arm and leads them near the church where Charlie's son had his funeral, back when I was a small girl stolen away in the late night by my father, there to see the other side of things, a lesson I keep on learning. Now the church has three walls and a door, but no roof yet. Mr. Darcey and the men get in a huddle and I know that Mr. Darcey's busy telling them about what he had to do to Mr. Prindergast. One by one, the men turn away and look toward Charlie's car, toward me inside his car, and I figure the least I can do is get out from behind the dirty glass and let myself be seen: Plenty Porter, the girl I am, the one who started this whole damn thing.

I take a few shaky steps away from the car and stop. Now that I'm outside, I don't know where I should be heading, so I look down at my feet and try to guess how many inches the dirt has traveled up my calves. Mr. Darcey, my grandfather, says, just loud enough for me to hear but soft enough so it doesn't sound like yelling, "Hey, Plenty, go on in and check on your friend. I'm sure he's coming round by now."

Looking up, I see that Mr. Darcey is smiling. Maybe he's doing it for me, to keep me calm, or maybe he is actually frightened to death himself, but whatever the reason for his smile, I feel a little bit better.

I can see Ed from outside the front door of the last house on the road. He's lying on top of a dining table, getting his forehead wiped down with a wet rag by a sweet-looking plump woman, old enough to be his mother. His color, which was always pale as milk anyway, seems to have come back some, and he breathes without too much effort. I don't recall seeing anyone else standing outside when I first walked up to the house, but I feel someone press gently against my back, encouraging me to go inside. "Go on, Plenty," Charlie says. "You're among friends now."

The plump woman with the wet rag sees me when I enter and leans down to whisper something into Ed's ear—something that makes him allow his head to roll to the side. Ed's eyes remain half closed, his lips parted only the smallest bit, but he manages, despite it all, to say, "Happy birthday, Plenty."

I woke up in someone else's bed, curled in a blanket next to Ed, who was still sleeping.

I don't remember being put to bed or even falling asleep, for that matter, but I am somehow aware of a time between falling asleep and waking—a time usually filled with dreams, but on this occasion was not. When I try to picture it, when I close my eyes and remember the time between falling asleep and waking, it is as dark as the day before you're born. And yet somehow, filled to the brim with life.

Ed is snoring loud like a man, which makes me giggle so much that I decide to get out of bed and let him sleep some more undisturbed. Climbing carefully out of the bed, I notice that my feet are pink and clean, even under the nails, and the knee that I scraped when I fell from Ed's tree has been covered with a small bandage. I wonder how it was someone did all this without giving me a tickle. Outside, it is somewhere between night and morning. Miles down the road, maybe somewhere outside of Illinois, in a place I might not ever get to see, sunlight is rolling toward us and will be here soon. But right now everything is hazy in a half-asleep sort of way.

Father's Dodge is parked next to Charlie's car. The door to the roofless church is open a bit. I dirty my feet by stepping down from the porch and onto the dew-soaked ground. The sweet-looking plump woman who had looked after Ed comes around the side of the church from the well, carrying with her a basket of damp rags. "Getting your feet dirty again, little miss?" she says. "Don't worry, we can can get 'em cleaned up before you leave."

"Who called my daddy?" I ask.

"Why, your grandpa did, of course," she says.

Walking inside the church, I get afraid of what Father is going to say when he sees me, after knowing all the trouble I caused. He lost his job and almost lost a daughter, all in the same day. And it gets me wondering which is worse. Mr. Darcey sees me when I walk through the door because he is sitting on a bench with Charlie, facing the back of the church. Father cranes his neck to see me enter, and stands as I move down the aisle toward him. Before I can say a single word, Father picks me up and I wrap my arms around his neck.

I'm not sure why exactly I start crying right then, but Father doesn't seem to mind much.

Charlie says, "Your daughter's a brave girl, Ray," and pats me on the back a couple of times.

I pull away so I can look at Father. "How'd he know your name, Daddy?" I ask.

"Because Charlie and I go back a long way, Plenty. Ever since he lost his boy."

"He's been my secret friend," I say.

"Not really, Plenty," Charlie says. "I called your daddy to tell him where he could find you when you came visiting me at the O."

"He did?" I ask Father.

"Of course he did," he says. I can see down onto the surface of Father's glasses, smudged and freckled with flakes of his skin. Pieces of us are always dying, sloughing off and falling like Marcie's hair, collected in folds of clothes, on pieces of glass. I take the glasses from off his nose and blow on them, cleaning them as best I can. I tell him, "It wasn't Mr. Darcey. It wasn't him visiting Marcie at the hospital all those times. He was telling the truth. It was Ed's pa all along."

"He knows, Plenty," Mr. Darcey says. "I told him everything."

Father lowers me down onto the bench next to him. "Listen real careful, Plenty." And sitting there next to him, with Mr. Darcey turning away almost like he was shy, Father starts talking to me about secrets, the kind that aren't lies, but ones that keep people from getting hurt—people like Mr. Darcey. "Your grandfather saved your life today, and this family will never be able to repay him for that kindness. But Mr. Prindergast was a very powerful man, a respected man, and it would be mighty hard to make people understand. Besides, your friend Ed should not grow up thinking ill against his father."

Before Father even finishes explaining, I already understand. Ed can't know that his father was bad because he should remember his father the way he always was to Ed, which was kind and gentle. Mr. Darcey couldn't have saved me because saving me involved stopping someone else from living. And people like Mr. Darcey, people who live like Charlie, in places separate from the rest, have not yet gotten to tell their side of the story.

Mr. Darcey sits down across from me when I invite

him to our house for breakfast—so he can see Mama, so we can tell her what her father did. And it is then that I promise not to tell anyone else what happened, and this time I do not sneeze.

And somehow in the course of being pulled into Mr. Darcey's arms, just as he begins to shake and let loose a lifetime's worth of tears onto my shoulder, I begin to see things clearly. The way things are in our family, they way things have changed. For a moment, Mr. Darcey's cries make a special sound. A sound like chirping; soft, breathless. And for a moment, it is Sadie that I hear coming from the feeble mouth of my grandfather. And somehow I know something about the future, as if it were revealed to me, as if God took a little breath just long enough for me to see:

Mr. Darcey will die next July while the rest of us watch fireworks. He will die on the porch of the tenant house, looking out on green hillsides. It will happen this way:

Mama leads him to his chair.

Mr. Darcey rocks.

And when his eyes fog over like glass, it is Mama who takes his hand.

Mr. Darcey says, "It's good to finally be with you in Ireland, my girl."

Mama says, "Yes, it is, Dad. It is."

24.

ONCE FATHER GOT ED up and out of bed and led him, all groggy and jelly-legged, to the car, most everyone who had gone back to bed was up again, ready to head off to the mill. And the ones who stayed up the whole of the night joined the others outside the church.

Mr. Darcey squeezes my shoulder when Father gets Ed inside the cab, knowing he will be coming for me next. But Father does not walk away from the Dodge, does not come and take my hand and lead me away from Mr. Darcey and the others. Instead, he leans against the front fender and crosses one leg over the other, content on waiting.

I glance up at Mr. Darcey, noticing for the first time the sparse curls of hair, checkered in shades of gray and brown, that sprout from underneath his chin. He smiles down on me and says, "You better go home, Plenty. Time to go home."

"Won't you be coming?" I ask.

"I'll be right behind you," he says. "Just want to get myself cleaned up first."

The thought of home settles like a lump in my throat that I can't seem to swallow. Everything up until now has been about *leaving* home, *looking* for a home big enough for someone like me—someone born into something hard, like the number eleven, one digit on the outside of ten.

Leaving the side of Mr. Darcey and the company of his neighbors, people who are now my friends just as Charlie has been all along—a friend to me, my grandfather, and father all at the same time—I think again about numbers, the number of steps it takes to get to my father standing at the Dodge, the number of ways in which I am a burden. And then I look back at the group of them, the ones standing next to the church, Mr. Darcey and Charlie and all of their friends and family, the people of Colored Town. I realize that where they live, how they live, has most to do with circumstance and misunderstanding. All along, Charlie and his friends were never allowed to have a home with the rest of the world, and yet they still gave one to my grandfather. And at that moment, I discover that I've never been the only one on the outside.

And at about the same time this thought comes to me, I know that my travels are over; that in one year and a night I moved across the surface of the entire country, and yet never left Illinois. In my mind's eye I imagine once again the map with all the roads that travel like rivers from one ocean to the other, winding across an entire country that suddenly seems unable to offer any more than I've already seen inside and around the Porter house. *Maybe,* I think. *Maybe a family can be the same thing as a country. Maybe both words can mean the same thing.*

When I reach Father, he palms the back of my head in his big, warm hand, and I somehow think of Mr. Prindergast, who was a father, who was Ed's father, who has left Ed behind. I look inside the cab of the truck and see that Ed is once again sleeping, slumped down on the bench, and I ask Father the only question left to ask. "What about Ed?" I say.

Father slides a hand under each of my arms and lifts me up into the cab, sitting me down right next to Ed, my friend. He answers simply, just before pushing shut the door:

"There's always room for one more."

Acknowledgments

It is important to first acknowledge my father, whose stories of growing up in Illinois have been, and continue to be, a great inspiration on my writing and non-writing life. My intense gratitude to Lisa Glatt for encouraging "Plenty" into a short story for her writer's workshop, and to Leelila Strogov for remembering it nearly two years later as she set off to create *Swink* magazine.

Thank you to Annie Zastoupil, Becky and Amy Aronson, and Jason Bitler for continually asking, early on, to read more pages when I was too embarrassed to show them. As far as friends go, no single word (let alone a book) could have been written without the patience and kindness of these listening ears: Paul Rees, Heather Dodd, and Steve Earley. There are none like you.

Thanks to my agent, Jonathan Pecarsky, for introducing me to the literary world. Without my incomparable editor, Tamar Brazis, and her gentle development, the final product would have left a lot to be desired. Thank you, Tamar, for making this such a fun and fulfilling project.

I am blessed by having family in great numbers. The Noonans and the Pelikans supported me from the beginning—so early on that I'm certain it wasn't clear it was deserved. Through the raising of their daughter (to whom this book is dedicated), my sister, Candace, and her husband, Eric, have redefined my understanding of love.

Lastly, I am forever indebted to my mother. Thank you for being a Pelikan and choosing a Noonan, and for making sure that only the best of those worlds entered our home. If this is a story about the power of family, then I am very lucky to know the meaning of the word.

About the Author

Brandon Noonan divides his time between Berkeley and Los Angeles, California, where he works as a screenwriter. He was born in Yuba City, California, which was, as he grew up, rated the worst city in America by Rand McNally. He is a graduate of the University of Southern California. This is his first novel.

This book was designed by Jay Colvin, who also created some of the art on the part titles. It is set in Mrs. Eaves, which was designed by Zuzana Licko to mimic the warmth and softness of old-fashioned letterpress printing.